The Evolution of Hallie Jo Everheart

Warmest Regards

Catherine Gray

The Evolution of Hallie Jo Everheart

—A NOVEL IN STORIES—

Catherine Grow

White River Press
Amherst, Massachusetts

Published by White River Press, Amherst, Massachusetts
whiteriverpress.com

ISBN: 978-1-935052-98-2

Book interior and cover design by Douglas Lufkin,
Lufkin Graphic Designs, Norwich, Vermont • www.LufkinGraphics.com

Black and white cover photo by John Vachon, Sept. 1939, from the Farm Security
Administration—Office of War Information Photograph Collection. Library of
Congress, Prints & Photographs Division, FSA/OWI Collection, LC-USF33-
001662-M5. Colorization of cover photo by Douglas Lufkin.

Library of Congress Cataloging-in-Publication Data

Names: Grow, Catherine, 1949- author.
Title: The evolution of Hallie Jo Everheart : a novel in stories /
    Catherine Grow.
Description: Amherst, Massachusetts : White River Press, [2023]
Identifiers: LCCN 2023001507 | ISBN 9781935052982 (paperback)
Subjects: LCGFT: Bildungsromans. | Linked stories.
Classification: LCC PS3607.R67855 E96 2023 | DDC 813/.6--dc23/eng/20230130
LC record available at https://lccn.loc.gov/2023001507

To Michael, my Rock

STORIES

Meeting Old Man Morrison

$\mathcal{I}$ WAS A SORRY SIGHT TO BEHOLD—just one pitiful little-girl-sized bundle of need and hurt. Well, who wouldn't be? Mama had died several months earlier, shortly after my ninth birthday. Since then, my days had been sadder than sad and my nights broken up by one hideous nightmare after another. I'd force myself out of bed each morning and grab whatever clothes I'd worn the day before—usually rumpled-up overalls, some sort of blouse or T-shirt, and a tattery old sweater—and put them on before doing what Mama'd called our morning ablutions. I'd look in the mirror over the sink in the bathroom, and my eyes would reflect back at me as dark and dead as lumps of coal in my pallid little-girl face.

My hair was hopeless. Though I tried to confine my curly red-gold mop into the braids Mama had always done up for me, they turned out a mess, even when I used barrettes to keep the stray tendrils in place. I looked so unkempt that several women around town had pointed at Pop and me and said, loud enough for God and everyone to hear, "What's the matter with the father? Doesn't he even *notice*?" Times like that, I prayed a hole would open up in the sidewalk and swallow me whole.

I, Hallie Jo Everheart, was going downhill fast, but neither Pop nor anyone else in my family seemed to pay attention or care—much less be able to help me or help much with anything else. Everything in our house was a disaster. Clothes spilled out of the hampers, and dishes piled up in the sink. Bedding grew stale and, in my brothers' cases, rank from God only knew what. The floors hadn't been vacuumed or swept or mopped in months; it'd been even longer since the furniture had been dusted. Before Mama died, I'd seen to some of this, but now I couldn't summon the will to even try.

And why should I? From the day I was born on April 29, 1951, my brothers—Eddie, now fourteen, and Drew, sixteen—always seemed to have it in for me. Don't ask me why. They devised ways to make me suffer when neither of our parents was looking. "You're a runt! A freak!" they'd snarl. "And such a *good girl*: a regular little kiss-up!" This hurt; all I'd ever wanted to do was help, because I believed that if I was good enough and helpful enough, Mama might not die.

When no one was looking, my brothers—large, savage, and strong—would pinch me. They'd also bump into me hard enough to make me stumble and sometimes topple over, making our parents wonder if I might be accident-prone or just plain clumsy.

How could I tell them? Mama and Pop had all they could handle trying to reclaim the dilapidated farm Mama had inherited from her Uncle Grant. Then Mama got cancer. Besides not wanting to bother my parents, I was afraid that being a tattletale would lead to even more abuse from my brothers. I tried to steer clear of them, but that didn't always work.

Pop was hopelessly overburdened—first, with trying against all odds to save Mama, and then, after her death, with keeping some semblance of order and sanity in our household as he stumbled into a future that never, in his worst nightmares, had he figured he'd have to face. He was so stricken by Mama's passing that he'd frequently retreat into his private world to try to fit enough fragments of his old self together to deal with matters he couldn't ignore—namely, keeping us children fed and clothed and with a roof over our heads while he tried to make a living farming the place that he and Mama had pledged their lives, their nest egg, their hopes, and their dreams to.

And Pop had other responsibilities. Besides farming, he was the pastor of Good Shepherd of the Ozarks, a small country church nearby, so he had to show up and deliver a sermon every Sunday morning. He also needed to continue writing essays and devotionals for several district and national religious journals to add extra money to our family's meager income. Some days he didn't bother to shave.

Though Pop tried his best to deal with our basic needs, I drifted through my days with scarcely a speck of comfort, care, or nurturing. I felt lost—so lost I worried that there was no way in Heaven or on Earth I'd ever find my way back.

In spite of it all, I figured Pop must be at least a little concerned about my well-being—and about my brothers' behavior toward me—because he refused to leave me at home, alone or with my brothers, whenever he had to leave the property.

That's how I met Old Man Morrison.

I was feeling shaky that Saturday morning when Pop made me go with him out to Morrison's place, so he could ask him what to do about our tractor that kept cutting out on him. Though I'd done my dead-level-best to stay steady after Mama died, I found it almost impossible to control my emotions; when I least expected it, tears would spill from the corners of my eyes and make my nose run. I'd be so embarrassed that I was anxious to avoid situations where people might ask why my eyes were so red and puffy.

And I certainly didn't have the desire or the energy—much less the words—to talk about the bottomless emotional pit that Mama's death had cast me into.

To say that meeting Old Man Morrison terrified me is an understatement. My brothers claimed that Old Man Morrison was peculiar, even scary and dangerous: definitely *not* someone you wanted to meet alone on a dark night. They said he lived by himself, half-wild and disheveled, in a dilapidated shack he'd thrown together in the woods far out of town, and that he'd just as soon kill you as look at you.

Classmates at my elementary school called him "The Boogeyman."

The name made me think of "Hansel and Gretel," with Old Man Morrison representing the witch in the story— who, if children like me should wander into her area, would lure them into her house, pop them into her oven, and bake and eat them, bit by tender, tasty bit.

But I was a sensible girl—at least I tried to be. I knew my brothers enjoyed frightening me, as did many of my classmates. I would have ignored their scare stories, except for the gossip I'd overheard outside the five-and-dime.

"Is that him?" Georgette Miller hissed, pointing to a tall, shabby-looking figure slipping into the hardware store. "Old Man Morrison?"

"Poor man," her mother, Cora, cooed.

"Poor man, my foot! That man's *dangerous!*"

"Oh? What do you know about him?" Irene Barkus asked, joining the conversation.

"Not much, except that he lives by himself in some ramshackle house out in the boondocks. Doesn't go to church or shop much. Hardly ever shows his face in town."

"Where'd he come from?"

"And what's he doing here in *our* town?"

"More to the point, what's he *hiding*? He's got to be running away from *something!*"

"No telling what that man might be up to!" the group concluded, clucking their tongues self-righteously.

It wasn't only the women who had misgivings about the man. "One strange customer" was the general consensus of the good ole boys who gathered at Dan Tucker's barbershop.

"Didn't that old guy used to run a machine and fix-it shop out on the edge of town?" Glen Owens would ask.

Heads would nod.

"What happened to it?" Tom Kinchloe would wonder.

"Couldn't make a go of it, I guess."

"Hell, the odd look of the guy and that twisted leg would scare most people off."

Affirmative grunts and nods would follow.

Through the years I'd heard enough such remarks that I couldn't help but feel frightened about the prospect of a face-to-face encounter. Still, I figured Pop would protect me from any serious harm. Besides, he needed advice about keeping our ancient Farm-All tractor in operation. In spite of all the suspicion about Old Man Morrison, local farmers and others who put little store in gossip knew he was a crack mechanic and jack-of-all-trades. There was apparently nothing under the sun that the man couldn't fix.

Pop called him "Slim," on account of his being so tall and lean. He was several inches taller than my father's six feet of height and without a doubt the skinniest man I'd ever seen—so thin that, in a brisk wind, I imagined he might be caught up like a dry leaf and blown into oblivion. This I could relate to because, by the time of our first meeting, I'd become almost gaunt myself. "She's skinny as a rail," I'd heard some women at Good Shepherd say about me. Well, what did they expect? Since Mama's death, I hadn't been able to eat much.

Pop wasn't much help. He had neither the time nor the energy to cook—much less the patience to coax me to eat. Our meals mostly consisted of dry stuff out of boxes or food warmed up from cans. Sometimes, he'd scramble some eggs, but they turned out hard, with crusty brown edges—nothing like the fluffy, buttery ones Mama used to make.

"Make sure your sister eats," he'd tell Drew and Eddie before he'd rush outside to do some farming chore. My brothers would barely lift a finger. Most times, I'd pick at whatever was set before me and do well to swallow a glassful of milk.

I hadn't wanted to go with Pop to Old Man Morrison's, but there was no way I could avoid it. Pop ushered me toward our pickup—a dilapidated aqua-blue Ford he'd picked up for a song—and settled me inside the cab. When seated, I brought my knees to my chest and leaned against the door, hoping my curled-up position would render me insignificant enough to protect me from the horrors of the outside world.

All too soon, we arrived at our destination.

Pop swung himself out of the truck and came around to my side. After wrenching the door open, he lifted me out of the cab and set me on my feet. I nervously rocked back and forth so precariously that he had to take me by the hand and guide me along the walkway to Old Man Morrison's garage.

At least that's where I thought we were going. With my head down, I couldn't see much ahead of me except for the dirt and gravel path, and eventually the bottom portion of a building built of weathered boards. The door to one of its bays had been pushed back to let in some light and air.

As we approached, I saw the lower half of a pair of faded Levi's and two scuffed leather work boots as a man with a pronounced limp walked through the door opening, vigorously wiping his hands with a rag. Four large dogs of indeterminate breed danced around the man, sniffing, snorting, and whining with eagerness to meet us strangers. Immediately, I was engulfed by wiggling, furry bodies vying with each other to be petted, until the man shooed the dogs into the yard.

"Howdy, Will," a froggy baritone rumbled. A large, bony hand reached out to clasp Pop's. "I heard. I'm sorry. Can't be easy."

"No," Pop replied softly.

There was a moment of silence before the boots shifted so that their toes were facing me. "And this is?"

"My daughter, Hallie."

I felt completely exposed—standing bare-naked with a giant spotlight shining down on me for the whole wide world to see. I wanted to shrink down to nothing.

Old Man Morrison scrutinized me. At first, he looked grouchy—as if he'd gotten up on the wrong side of the bed that morning—but then his expression softened as if, in spite of my pitiful looks and shyness, there was something about me that he might find interesting.

His hand—clean but grease-stained, with a residue of grime under the nails—extended downward to greet me. In the process, I noticed that with its bones and muscles and veins it looked like a relief map of the hills and valleys and rivers of our local Ozark landscape. The arm rising above a knobbly wrist was covered by a threadbare plaid flannel shirt. I felt nervous, but gathered enough courage to place my hand into Old Man Morrison's. A second hand, deeply scarred, reached out, and cupped my hand with surprising delicacy. "Hallie," the man repeated, making my name sound like a melody.

I couldn't speak, and I was afraid to look up at him, but something compelled me to. The man's hair was scraggly, his face long, thin, and creased with wrinkles. He looked as if he had at least a week-old stubble of beard. Another deep scar ran the length of one of his prominent cheekbones, lending a pirate-ish aspect to his appearance. I caught my breath, more from fascination than fear—although from the comments I'd heard around town there might be plenty to fear.

His eyes—light turquoise and framed by bushy gray eyebrows—met mine with such directness that I felt unnerved. "This," he said pointing to the scar on his face, "doesn't do much to improve my looks, but I guarantee you

I'm not as scary as I look." He seemed amused, and his smile, though slightly crooked, was gentle.

And there was more. Behind that smile I sensed that there was something buried deep inside this peculiar man—something like the pain and loneliness I'd been feeling. But how could that be? He was an adult—sixty-ish to Pop's forty-four years—and I was just a kid—a nine-year-old girl.

"You okay?" Old Man Morrison asked gruffly. I nodded. "You sure? You're not frightened?"

I shook my head so emphatically that the braids I'd done up for myself that morning whipped against my shoulders and threatened to come undone. "That's good," he said. "You look like you're a brave girl—one who isn't spooked by appearances. Still, you look like you're feeling a little puny."

"She's not only *feeling* puny, she *is* puny," Pop added. "I can't get her to eat. Past few weeks, she's dropped more weight than I care to think about. Worries me to death."

Old Man Morrison knelt down on one knee beside me, his lame leg stretched out at an angle. "Feeling low, are you?" he asked in as calm and comforting a voice as a beat-up-looking, crotchety old man could manage. "I'm sorry about your mother," he said. He talked to me in the tone of respect he would have used with an adult. "You know, this is probably the worst thing you'll ever have to go through. One of the worst, at least. You get yourself through this, and you'll be able to get through anything."

I forced myself to keep eye contact with him but bit my lower lip to hold back tears.

"It's okay to cry," Old Man Morrison said. "The death of your mother is definitely something worth crying about." He pulled a blue and white bandanna handkerchief from his back pocket and offered it to me. "Take your time getting over it, and don't let anybody rush you. You've got to find your own way in your own time."

He maneuvered himself haltingly back onto his feet, then turned to Pop. "Give her time, Will. She's not gonna up and die on you. But she's going to need some help getting herself together and figuring out where to go. Eventually—probably sooner than later—her appetite'll pick up, and so will her spirits." He looked down at me. "Won't they, Hallie?"

I nodded, hesitantly.

"I don't know . . . " Pop began.

"Sure they will," Morrison said. "In time, she'll catch hold and begin to thrive." He looked at me again. "Won't you?"

"I guess so," I stammered. With Pop and him standing beside me, I was already beginning to lose some of my anxiety.

"And let's face it," he added, "she still has a ways to go before she's as skinny as me!"

So far, Old Man Morrison didn't seem anything like what my brothers and the local townspeople had made him out to be. Could they be wrong?

I decided they must be crazy. Or just plain stupid. Anybody but a grade A fool could see beyond the limp and scars and realize that this strange-looking man wasn't the monster they claimed he was.

Then and there, I decided to take a chance. I collected myself and asked with a boldness that surprised me, "Sir, what's your name? What's your real name? People just call you Old Man Morrison."

Pop pushed his glasses up the bridge of his nose and stared hard at me. It'd been a long time since I'd shown much interest in anything in the world around me.

"I mean . . . er . . . the other one isn't very nice . . . and it just doesn't seem to fit."

"My full name is Jared Tyler Morrison," he said. Not many people know that—or care."

"Is it okay if I call you Mr. M?"

"Sounds fine to me," he said. "It'll be your special name for me, one that nobody else uses. I've been called a lot of names. Some, like Slim, are nicer than others. But generally I don't pay much mind to what people call me, so long as it's not late for dinner." He chuckled, "And despite my scrawny appearance, I do eat plenty of dinner."

With introductions out of the way, Mr. M led Pop and me along the walkway to his house and ushered us in through the back door, down a hallway, and into a large living room. "Why don't you sit here?" he said, guiding me to a comfortable-looking wing chair covered in a lovely dusty-rose shade of velvet.

Sitting down, I looked around the room while the men talked. The walls were painted an off-white color and trimmed with dark unpainted wood. Thick lace curtains dressed a pair of front windows. Above me, dark wood beams spanned the width of the ceiling. A wide-board floor was uncovered except for a braided rug in front of the fireplace.

Unlike the hodge-podge of modern stuff in our living room at home, this room was full of furniture from another era: ancient, beat-up pieces that radiated warmth and history and came together to create a harmonious whole. Everything about the room exuded antiquity and spoke of a life lived deeply and with a simple, quiet elegance.

Sitting there, I felt myself melting into the surroundings. A grandfather clock tick-tocked like a heartbeat. A large fireplace with a cast-iron heat stove dominated one wall of the room. To the right were bookshelves filled with volumes of varying heights and widths. There was also a spinet piano and matching bench. "How in the *world* does a man like him have a piano?" I wondered.

Fragments of music that Mama used to play on our old upright at home drifted through my mind along with part of a lullaby she used to sing to me at bedtime. Waves of longing suddenly welled up in me, and tears gathered behind my eyelids. "Not here. Not now," I told myself.

As I continued to survey the room, I noticed a corner cupboard filled with old china and pretty colored glasses of various shapes. "There's more to this man than meets the eye," I thought.

M's living room. Mr. M's cat was perched, as I'd first seen her, atop the sofa.

I scrunched deeper into the sofa and closed my eyes, half dozing until I became aware that someone was near.

Opening my eyes, I was almost scared out of my wits. Mr. M was standing directly over me. "So you're awake," he said.

I sat bolt upright, drawing my knees to my chest. "Where am I?"

"You're inside the house," Mr. M said.

"Where's Pop?" my voice trembled.

"He had to run some errands. I told him he should let you sleep—God knows you needed it—and that you'd be fine here with me."

"But how did I get inside?" I quavered.

"It got cloudy, so your father carried you in," Mr. M told me. "You were so sound asleep you barely moved when he put you on the sofa. Even though we were still talking, he couldn't budge you."

"When's he coming back?"

"Pretty soon."

"Soon?" I thought. "*Soon?*" But why had Pop left me here at all? I was alone in a strange house with this strange, odd-looking man. He seemed nice, but I still didn't know him well enough to lower my guard. Anything could happen.

I looked at the figure looming over me and didn't move a muscle. "What's he going to do to me?" I wondered. "Am I now going to find out why they call him 'The Boogeyman' after all?" My heart was beating double-time.

"Don't be afraid," Mr. M said. "I wouldn't hurt you."

Easy for him to say. I remained cautious. "How long have I been here?" I said, holding myself rigid.

"A good long while."

I groaned and shifted my weight. Mr. M noticed my movement and took a cue from it. "Come with me," he said. "I've got something to show you."

"Not in a million years," I thought, remembering how Mama had told me never to go anyplace with a stranger—or maybe she'd said not to accept a ride or candy?

It was all too much for me.

I didn't say a word but flinched when Mr. M grasped the top of the afghan and pulled it off of me. I shivered, wondering what in Heaven's name was about to happen. I felt trapped like a bird flying into the sides of its cage, desperate to get out. Mr. M held out a hand, which I had no choice but to take.

I felt wobbly—almost frightened enough to faint—but Mr. M pulled me onto my feet and steadied me. Then, with a hand gripping my shoulder, he walked me slowly out of the room.

"Where're we going?" I whimpered.

"You'll see."

I let myself be pulled along and found myself being led down the hallway and into a kitchen painted a soft shade of yellow that reminded me of the daffodils and sunshine of spring. Ahead of me was a square table; on it was a small parcel, wrapped in brown paper and tied with string.

Mr. M guided me to the table, pulled out a chair, and instructed me to sit down. He gestured toward the package. "Open it."

My hands shook so much that my fingers were clumsy. Mr. M behaved as if he had all the time in the world.

The wrapping opened to reveal a book. But not just any book; it was a manual written for children and other novices who were serious about learning to draw. Within its pages was a wealth of instructions in easy-to-understand illustrations and language.

I began thumbing through the pages. "I got this for you," Mr. M said.

I looked up at him. "For me? To keep?"

"Yes, Ma'am."

"You got this book 'specially for me?"

A smile twitched the corners of Mr. M's mouth. "I thought it might come in handy."

"It does. It will. But why did you get it for me?"

Mr. M seated himself and took my hands into his. He looked serious, life-and-death serious. "Making art can save you," he said with great conviction. "It can—it *will*—take you out of yourself and away from the problems you're facing."

I sat quietly, captivated by what the man had just said.

He continued, "You need to keep drawing, Hallie. You've got talent and potential. Whatever else you do or don't do in your life, you ought to continue making art." He paused to clear his throat before saying, "Promise me you will."

"I will," I whispered.

"Say it again; say it so I can hear you," Mr. M commanded.

"I will! I will!"

"Good!" The man seemed to be satisfied. Or was he?

I reopened the book, preparing to look through its pages more thoroughly, when, once again, Mr. M's hands covered mine. I looked up, startled.

"Now, you need to do something for me," he said, sounding almost severe.

Fear shot through my body. "What?" I could barely keep my voice steady.

Without a word, Mr. M pushed up from his chair and made his way to the stove. He lifted the lid of a large pot and stirred its contents. A rich-smelling steam rose from it.

"What're you cooking?" I asked.

"Beef stew. And you're going to eat some."

"I am?"

"You are," the man replied brusquely.

And so I did.

I was on my second bowl when Pop returned. Mr. M went out to greet him, then brought him down the hallway and into the kitchen. There, my father stopped and stared at me. "What's this?" he said, clearly astounded.

"Beef stew," I chirped.

Pop looked questioningly at Mr. M.

"It's delicious!"

"Actually, it's not all that special," Mr. M demurred. "It's just a plain, basic meat, carrots, onions, and potatoes stew. I make big pots of it at a time, so I can freeze some to eat later. "

"But you got her to *eat*," Pop said, his voice straining with emotion.

"All she needed was a nudge."

I emptied my bowl and pointed to the book beside me. "Look what else Mr. M gave me. It'll show me how to be an artist."

Pop picked up the book and examined it. "It certainly will." He then turned to Mr. M. "Where'd you find this?"

"I stopped by the Oldest Hills bookstore and picked up a copy a couple of days ago when I was in town.

"You went to all that trouble? Just for Hallie?"

"Wasn't any trouble," Mr. M replied softly.

"Well, I certainly want to reimburse you for it."

Mr. M stared at Pop as if he'd lost his senses. "I'm going to pretend I didn't hear that," he said. "Besides, you've got plenty of other things to deal with."

"I do." Pop glanced at me. He motioned his head in my direction. "But it looks like there might be one less now that you've gotten her to eat."

"*If* she continues to eat," Mr. M said with an edge to his voice. "To make sure, you'd better take the rest of this stew home with you."

"Thanks but no thanks, Slim," Pop protested. "We don't need any food handouts yet."

"Will, this is something you *need* to do—for the girl's sake."

I was shocked. I'd never heard anyone talk to Pop like that! Still, it was obvious my father needed help, and so did I. And Mr. M was doing what needed to be done.

He'd already pulled the pot of stew off the stove and was preparing to wrap it in thick towels when I sidled up to him, took his hand, and brought it to my face. I rested my cheek against the scarred and bumpy back of it. "Thank you," I said. "Thank you for everything."

Mr. M rubbed his hand back and forth across my cheek. "It's okay," he said. "It's okay." He then turned, finished wrapping the stew pot in the towels, and sent Pop and me on our way.

That night, I ate more of the stew—ate until I thought I would burst. And full of that good, solid nourishment, I slept soundly.

And though I would continue to grieve for Mama, I, Hallie Jo Everheart, began to find my way back to life.

Filling In for Mama

I T WAS FOUR MONTHS past my twelfth birthday and, like it or not, I, Hallie Jo Everheart, was being pulled into adolescence.

I was also being pulled deeper into helping maintain what was left of the farm Mama had inherited from her Uncle Grant. We had moved there five years ago, a year and a half before Mama became ill and died. Cancer. Breast. Doctors caught it too late. There was nothing any of us could do except try to make her comfortable and watch while she faded away to nothing before our eyes.

Life hadn't been the same since Mama's passing, a few months after I turned nine. Since then, I'd been trying to do all that was humanly possible to fill in for her so our lives could stay as steady as possible. For his part, Pop remained dedicated to living the agrarian life he and Mama had chosen, but he wasn't experienced in raising animals or farming crops. When problems arose, he'd take it personally and fall into dark moods—during which gloom filled the house like a thick, gray fog. The walls and ceilings virtually wept with it. He'd sit in a chair for hours, gazing out the living room window. When I tried to check on him, he'd continue staring, as if he didn't even know I was there. If the weather was pleasant, he might rouse himself and head out to our pond.

The pond was Pop's sanctuary, a half-acre of weedy water that held within its depths a mix of catfish, perch, blue gills, and frogs. He'd sit on the bank, holding his Zebco rod and reel and fish for hours—so long that I'd sometimes take a pitcher of lemonade and a hat out to him. More often than not, he looked bewildered when I arrived, as if I'd jarred him back from some far-away place in his mind where I didn't even exist. "Here, Pop," I'd say, setting my offerings beside him. He'd nod, and I'd slip away, so he could return to wherever he'd been. He'd always throw back anything he caught.

Though I gave it everything I had, there was really no way I could fill in for Mama. Neither could anyone else. Not that Pop ever bothered to find out. You'd have thought that after a proper period of mourning, he might've gone looking for a new woman. It wouldn't have been difficult. Pop was good-looking and, at forty-seven, not too terribly old.

He was six feet tall and well built: slim, but muscular, with broad shoulders, a hard, flat belly, and narrow hips that looked terrific in Levi's. Dressed in his coat and tie to preach a sermon at Good Shepherd of the Ozarks, the church where he was a pastor, he was downright handsome.

His hair, a rich chestnut brown, was only beginning to show strands of silver. His eyes, a clear cobalt blue, looked out at the world seriously and straightforwardly, though they seemed to transform into shades of slate or ebony when something angered or upset him. After years of hard work, his face was becoming weathered. He had what a person might call "rugged good looks" and would have been a fine catch for any woman.

But he didn't look for one. Though Lydia Jessup and Maria Thomas always lingered to talk with him after church—and I know any number of women around town would have given their eye teeth to become better acquainted with him—Pop had decided to devote his time and energy to running the farm and raising me and my brothers, Drew and Eddie, so that we would grow up the way Mama would have wanted. This, Pop said, was all the responsibility he wanted for the foreseeable future. Fine, except that I had to take up the slack that Mama's absence had left in our lives.

The lack of any maternal presence in the family made me feel lonely and desolate. Every morning, after I'd pull on my hand-me-down overalls and a blouse or T-shirt and braid my unruly reddish-gold hair into a single long plait, I'd make my way downstairs, then down the hallway and into Pop's office. I'd usually find him asleep, his head resting on the piles of invoices on his old oak desk or slumped in his decrepit overstuffed rocking chair in the far corner of the room. I'd tiptoe up to him and gently prod his shoulder. "Morning, Pop," I'd say. He'd wake up, vaguely disoriented and feeling for his glasses.

I'd bring him a mug of coffee and—on the rare occasions when he felt conversational—we'd talk. I'd perch on the arm of the chair and he'd steady me with a sideways hug. I'd feel his breath blowing through my hair like warm gusts of an early summer breeze and I'd feel like nothing terrible could ever happen.

But terrible things did happen.

The fact was that we Everhearts were barely making ends meet on our farm. The only steady income we had was from Pop's preaching and what he earned from writing columns for various religious magazines. Though we grew most of our own food, we still weren't producing enough to make any money selling surpluses. No one in our family was suffering, but things were definitely tight.

And tense. In the three years since Mama's death we'd experienced what our good friend, Mr. M—Jared Tyler Morrison—called a "run of bad luck." Shortly after Mama's death, my brothers stopped helping on the farm and took jobs in town. Then we had sick and dying rabbits, followed by Pop's falling ill with a mysterious lung disease that had lasted for months. After that, we'd been hit with other misfortunes. After each disaster, Pop became increasingly disheartened and withdrawn.

And now there was the problem with the geese. Five of them had shown up one morning on our pond. Ordinarily, we might have welcomed an addition to our livestock, but shortly after their arrival, the geese began crossing over into our neighbor Merle Hazlett's property to pillage his crops. Every day about mid-morning, I would see them from my bedroom window upstairs, their plump, white shapes gliding across the surface of the pond looking like fluffy meringues on some fancy dessert. They looked picturesque and serene, but then when no one was looking, the birds would head single-file into our neighbor's corn fields.

Something had to be done, seeing as how Mr. Hazlett kept phoning to complain. At first, he was polite—probably because Pop was a man of the cloth. Pop would apologize and promise to take care of the problem. And he tried. God knows, he tried! First, the two of us built up the fence around the pond in an effort to contain the geese. Then we reinforced the bottom of the fence by burying small-gauge chicken wire a foot into the ground so the geese couldn't squeeze out underneath.

But there was no fencing them in. Those geese always found ways to escape and feast on our neighbor's crops.

After a few weeks of this, Hazlett's patience ran out. "Damn it, Everheart!" he bellowed over the phone. "Them geese is in my corn again! Hard earned cash down the gullets of them god-damned, stinkin' bastards!" He yelled so loudly that I could hear his voice clear across the kitchen by the sink where I was washing up the supper dishes. I wrung out the dishrag, draped it over the faucet, and ambled across the room to lean against the wall next to the phone, listening to fragments of the conversation and hoping my presence might offer Pop moral support.

"I think I'm a patient man," Hazlett kept on, his voice lowering somewhat. "You been promisin' to take care of 'em—and I know you been tryin'—but them geese is still in my corn! That's my livelihood, man! You gotta do somethin' about it . . . and damn quick!" There was a fit of coughing at his end of the line, then a *harrumph*. "I don't wanta cause trouble, but . . . well . . . *shoot* the bastards, if you hafta. Or else I'll call the sheriff."

Shooting the geese was the last thing in the world Pop wanted to do, but there seemed to be no other way to stop them; they couldn't abide being confined. The day Pop decided to get rid of them, I accompanied him as far as the pasture gate. His shotgun—a twelve-gauge pump he borrowed from Mr. M—looked awkward in his hand, and he held it away from his body as if he were transporting a dead skunk. He gave me a pitiful look when I swung the gate closed behind him, as if he himself was staring death in the face. I climbed the sturdy metal slats and watched him while he shuffled through the field, his bare head bobbing above the tall grass that had turned brown and brittle in the blistering late August sun. Our area hadn't had any rain to speak of for months, so everything was parched. The well water was so low that Pop had warned us to take care how we used it.

When I could no longer see Pop from my lookout atop the gate, I sprinted back into the house and upstairs to my bedroom. From the window I could see Pop, still moving slowly down the tamped path that led to the pond. I watched as he shoved one of our sows, curious and nosing up to him, out of the way with the tip of the gun. He had to do this again and again, because that sow just wouldn't quit.

There'd never been any love lost between Pop and our sows—call it temperamental differences, though who in the world could warm up to an animal that might roll on its own young and occasionally eat them? Nevertheless, the beasts had the potential to earn us a decent chunk of cash-money.

What had been a fairly impersonal dislike intensified when, one morning a year or so before the arrival of the geese, Pop found Cookie dead outside the barn.

How he'd loved that mongrel pup! He'd discovered her, skinny and starving, scavenging through garbage at a truck stop where he'd stopped one day for coffee and a cheeseburger on the way back from a meeting in Jeff City. He'd coaxed her into his pickup with bits of burger and brought her home. She filled out nicely—looked like a cross between a cocker and a collie—and was Pop's constant companion.

Cookie had been killed by something; what, we never really knew. Pop said it might have been the one old sow that always pushed through the gate when we forgot to latch it securely; invariably, it would get into the yard and the feed house. One afternoon it'd demolished three sacks of corn and nosed into a couple of others before Pop and I returned from running errands in town.

It's a wonder Pop didn't go after that sow when Cookie was killed, but nobody knew for sure if that's what got her. Any number of culprits could have done it. Strange, though, that the dog's body had no open wounds or broken bones or any other signs of a struggle.

Pop's life seemed to fall apart after that. It was almost as bad as the period right after Mama died. For weeks, he sat in his easy chair in the living room, feet propped on the ottoman, staring into space. If I asked him a question, he'd respond with a one-word answer. I managed to persuade him to eat something every day, but he wouldn't take much. It was as if he'd given up on life.

And worse: he seemed to be losing his good Christian faith, mumbling to himself about how maybe there wasn't a God after all—at least not one he could believe in anymore. How could there be? No just and merciful God would have allowed a good woman like Mama to die or his faithful servants to suffer and struggle in the face of disaster after disaster.

Occasionally, I got downright angry with Pop, to say nothing of my resentment of my brother Eddie, who was still living at home but did nothing to help. What did they expect from me? I was still only a kid—not even a teenager—trying to do both a man's and a woman's jobs helping take care of the farm, the house, and the family. Inwardly, I raged at my brother for refusing to lift a finger and wondered how Pop could sit there and mope when there was so much to be done. Didn't he realize he had responsibilities? Why was I being stuck with so much of the work?

Outside, while I was feeding the livestock or weeding our vegetable gardens, I'd carry on a conversation with God. "Why," I'd beseech the Almighty, "do I have to do it *all*? Why am I taking care of *Pop* instead of *him* taking care of *me*?" Then, I'd feel ashamed. After all, I was a big girl now—twelve years old—and Mama would expect me to manage things no matter what.

At night, I'd fall asleep as soon as my head hit my pillow, only to jar awake later, almost too achy to move, crying from nightmares in which Mama would accuse me of not taking care of the family the way I'd promised to do when she was so ill.

I remembered those times vividly: smoothing Mama's face which had become so thin that her skin felt as soft and filmy as gossamer. Her hair—a lighter colored version of my reddish-blond mop—was stubbly as it grew back after the radiation treatments and chemotherapy. As sick as she was, she'd have me lie down next to her and pull me so close to her that the bones of her poor, emaciated body would feel knobbly against my little-girl frame. She would look at me and say, "I'm afraid you're going to have to be the woman of the house soon. Your father and brothers are going to have to have somebody to look after them."

"Mama, you're not going to die, are you?" I'd sob. "You're not going to die?"

"Promise me," Mama would say, wiping the tears from my face.

"But, Mama, I don't *want* you to die! I don't *want* you to die!"

She would then cup my face between her hands and murmur, "No matter what happens to me, never forget how much I love you. You are my own dear girl." She'd kiss me on the forehead and repeat, "Now promise me."

I'd nod, having no idea what this was going to mean: the grinding day-to-day responsibilities of trying to fill my mother's role and the guilt I'd feel when I couldn't manage to do it successfully. Sometimes Pop would appear in my dreams, shaking his head sadly and whispering, "I'm sorry, Hallie Jo. I don't love you anymore." Mornings, I'd wake up puffy-eyed and too exhausted to get out of bed. But I knew I had to. Who else would get breakfast and keep the place going?

One day, I walked into the living room and asked Pop straight out, "Don't you love me anymore? Don't you even care?" Pop's face immediately crumpled. Then, without a word, he rose, stiff as an old man, and shuffled out of the room. He continued down the hallway, disappeared into his office, and closed the door. I tiptoed after him and put my ear against it. I thought I heard him crying. I began to cry, too. At first, my sobs were as indistinct as Pop's. When they deepened to a wail, I ran outside and climbed into the branches of my favorite oak—a gnarly old giant behind the barn—and stayed there until I cried myself out. Then I hurried back to the house. It was nearly suppertime. I had no idea what to fix, and soon everyone would file in, expecting food.

When I arrived, Pop was making sandwiches. He told me not to worry; that we'd eat picnic-style that night. Later, he sat me down, and we discussed the difficulties we'd faced trying to make a living on the farm. "But I'm far from licked,"

Pop assured me. "And no matter what happens, I won't stop loving you."

But that was before the problem with the geese began. With a final shove and a yell loud enough to carry all the way back to the house, Pop pushed the sow away. He unhooked a section of the fence surrounding the pond and stepped onto the lip of the land that surrounded the water. By now, I could barely see him. In his khaki work shirt and faded Levi's, he pretty well blended into the background of scraggly buck-brush and dusty brown earth. The cream-colored geese stood out boldly against the murky green of the pond. "God," I began a whispered prayer, "please don't let him shoot himself."

I couldn't bear to watch anymore so I busied myself cleaning cobwebs from the corner of the bedroom. Soon I heard two loud gunshots. Then another and another and another.

"How can he do it?" I asked myself. This was Pop, who couldn't bear to hurt any living creature. He kept no weapons of his own around the farm and insisted we catch spiders and other large insects in a Mason jar and set them free outside.

But he had to do it—had to get rid of the geese somehow—and there didn't seem to be any other way.

When the fencing didn't work, Pop had tried to herd the geese up from the pond and corral them into a pen near the barn. He figured the best time to carry out his plan would be just before dusk. The impudent creatures would be full of Hazlett's corn by then and settled near the pond, fat, content, and not inclined to flight. "No, I do *not* need help!" he bristled at my offer of assistance. "I can take care of this myself. Just leave me alone to do what needs doing."

But that plan, too, came to nothing, because the geese weren't inclined to be herded. That's when Pop concluded that there was nothing else to do but shoot them. And now he'd gone out and done it—or so I thought.

When I heard the gunshots, I tried to block the visions inside my head of shotgun shells exploding into the sides of the poor wild creatures, followed by widening pools of scarlet on the surface of the pond.

And then, all of a sudden, I heard Pop's steps on the porch. Entering the kitchen, he put the shotgun down, and announced he might have winged one or two of the birds but that he'd scared the living daylights out of all of them. He said he'd seen them disappear into our woods and didn't think they'd ever return to the pond or Hazlett's field again.

This turned out to be wishful thinking, however, because sure enough, two days later, we spotted the geese again preening their feathers beside the pond. "Damn it," Pop said. "Why couldn't the damn things take off for good like those dumb young turkeys did?"

I remembered the episode with the turkeys all right: combing the woods for hours, looking for five chicks that had pushed beneath the poultry house fencing. We never did find them. Why the geese didn't just fly away, I'll never know. I guess all that corn next door was too good to pass up.

Late that afternoon, we got another angry phone call from Mr. Hazlett. I heard Pop trying to placate him. After he hung up, he paced the kitchen floor, his hands flexing and un-flexing nervously. "I guess I'm going to have to get serious and kill the stupid things once and for all," he said.

"Too bad we can't just give them away," I mumbled.

Pop stopped in his tracks. "What'd you say?"

"I said, 'Too bad we can't just *give* 'em away.'"

"That's it! That's *it!*" Pop grabbed my shoulders and gave them a shake. He went straight to the phone book, then dialed *The Plainfield Journal* to advertise: "Five adult geese— free for the asking. Call Reverend William J. Everheart, 436-7802." "Why I didn't think of this before, I'll never know," he said jubilantly. "It's a perfect solution—if it works."

A day or two later, as I was peeling potatoes for supper, I answered a phone call from a woman eager to take the geese off our hands—for free. "I'll be by in an hour to pick them up," she said. Pop and I immediately stopped what we were doing and headed down to the pond to try to round up the geese.

As we approached, the birds—too stuffed with corn to fly—ducked under a bank of bramble bushes bordering the pond. "Ssshhhttt!" Pop sputtered. He instructed me to crawl beneath the brambles, grab each goose, and haul it out so he could put it in a gunnysack.

No sooner had I crawled under the first bush than I felt something rip. "Shoot!" I said under my breath, using a sanitized version of the word I suspected Pop had uttered a few moments earlier. Without looking, I knew that I'd just torn my blouse—the extra-special one with the hand-embroidered rosettes along the neckline that Mama's best friend, Margaret, had sent from California for Mama's last birthday. Mama had worn it once or twice before she became completely bedridden. She'd then given it to me to wear when I grew older, telling me that she couldn't bear to have something that lovely hidden away in a drawer. For some reason, I had put it on that afternoon with my newest pair of shorts to see if it fit. The blouse was still too large, but I'd left it on anyway, because it made me feel grown up and pretty. Also, for some odd reason, I'd felt shaky all day and wanted to feel Mama close to me. Not for a moment did I think I would end up belly-down in muck, scrambling after geese. I cursed the fact that there'd been no time to change into my usual T-shirt and overalls before we rushed to the pond.

I kept crawling, full of resentment for having to go into the underbrush at all. Couldn't Pop see I was growing up and this was no fit activity for a respectable young woman—especially one who was working so hard to keep the house running just like Mama had?

The geese twisted and squirmed and honked and pecked. Everywhere I turned my hair got snared on branches and tangled with leaves and twigs. My arms and legs became smeared with goose droppings and crisscrossed with scratches. Sweat got into the scratches and made them sting. I was furious. *Fure-ee-ous!*

And there was something else: a dull ache, throbbing low in my belly. It had gone on the entire day, and I felt as if I was starting to get sick, but not exactly. My breasts—what there was of them—were sore, too, and itchy almost to distraction. Crawling in all that filth didn't help. After what seemed like an eternity, we captured all the geese and lugged them up from the field.

As we approached the house, a stout woman in a red checkered blouse and snug-fitting Levi's jumped out of a battered pickup and began pulling crates out of its bed. She straightened up when we came near, then smoothed her blouse and ran a hand over her crisp, jet-black curls. "Hi, I'm Mae Daniels," she said, striding toward Pop and holding out a tough farmwoman's hand.

"You have no idea the pleasure, Ma'am," Pop said, shaking her hand and looking at her as if she was offering him salvation.

"But what about me?" I said to myself. Didn't all my efforts and care and consideration count for anything? Why was Pop looking at this woman that way—someone he didn't even know, someone who had never helped him one lick, when I'd been killing myself for years, helping him on the farm, trying to fill in for Mama?

"Just put 'em in there," she instructed with a jerk of her head toward the crates. I stayed put. What right did *she* have to order me around like that? Pop frowned at me and gestured for me to do as I was told.

"That your girl?" she asked Pop, smiling. He nodded, smiling right back. "Whatcha been doin', honey? Rollin' in the mud?" she asked and then added "Uh-oh! Looks like you tore your blouse." She turned to Pop, shaking her head and chuckling, "Tomboy girls! Aren't they somethin'?" I didn't like the way she was talking to my father like that—like an equal, too familiar, and sort of flirty-like.

Pop nodded in agreement, failing to mention that I'd worked hard and gotten dirty helping *him* capture *her* geese for her and that I was *not* a tomboy but the woman of the house. I looked down. The tear across the front of Mama's blouse was a foot long, and the whole blouse was smeared with mud and droppings. "Damn!" I shouted. "God damn!"

The two adults stopped talking and stared at me. Pop looked shocked. Fortunately, I'd already closed the gap in the front of the blouse so that no one could see anything. Fighting back tears, I stumbled back to the house, seething all the way. *Why* had Pop let this woman insult me? Why hadn't he *stuck up* for me? He could have at least *explained!* He's my *father*, for God's sake; it's his job to *defend* me!

And what about everything I'd been doing around our place? Didn't that deserve at least some recognition and some appreciation?

I stomped into the house and down the hall and into the bathroom. I slammed the door so hard the frame rattled. Then I yanked off the blouse. "Damn! Damn! God *damn!*" I screamed. I knew I was going against Pop's teaching by taking the Lord's name in vain, but it felt good. Damned good! I was sick to death of following his rules and working so hard to take care of everything and everybody. Besides, I figured that the Almighty would excuse my blasphemy under the circumstances.

I wadded the ruined blouse into a ball and threw it into a corner with so much force that my knuckles cracked. Next I wriggled out of my dirty shorts and filthy sneakers, then the white lace bra and matching panties I'd fought mightily to convince Pop to let me order from the Sears Roebuck catalog. I hurled the bra into the corner and picked up the panties, getting ready to do the same, when I noticed a rust-colored stain.

My scalp prickled. Then I felt queasy. I'd heard about this. Two years earlier, all the girls in my grade had been given booklets. That stain could mean only one thing: I was now, at least physically, becoming a woman.

But I didn't want to become a woman—not now, not yet. I needed someone to console me, to help and advise me about all this. "Mama!" something whimpered inside me. "Mama! Mama! Mama!"

But Mama wasn't there. She hadn't been there for years and never would be. I was the only female in the family, and I'd have to handle this by myself. It certainly wasn't something I could discuss with Pop.

But who could I talk to? It'd have to be a woman. . . but not just any woman. It surely wouldn't be somebody like Mae Daniels, who was more interested in trying to charm Pop and insult me.

I shuffled to the tub, swatted back the shower curtain, and turned the water on, full-blast. With shaking fingers, I loosened my hair, then shook it out, combing my fingers through it. A mass of stray leaves and twigs dislodged and fell onto the linoleum; I kicked them aside. I turned and glanced at my face in the mirror. There were more freckles than I'd remembered, as well as a long, ugly scratch across one cheek. My eyes were large and round and clear blue like Mama's, but I was so worn out it looked as if I had bruises beneath them. "Ugly," I thought. "Not beautiful like Mama."

Then suddenly, cruelly, it hit me: I *wasn't* Mama and never could be. Try as I might, there was no way I could actually take Mama's place or fill in for her. I couldn't be anyone other than my own anxious, uncertain, self-conscious twelve-year-old self. Who that self was, I had no idea. I guessed I'd just have to wait and find out.

I stepped into the tub and pulled the curtain closed. Then I released the shower and let water stream all over my body. It beat on my back and shoulders and spilled onto my front. It drummed on my head and saturated my scalp. I grabbed my bottle of Prell and poured a viscous green puddle of it into my hand. I lathered my hair and rinsed it, inhaling the sweet fragrance of the shampoo and watching the suds cascade down my arms, concealing, for a moment, all the scratches. Suds bubbled around the swells of my breasts, past my belly, and between my legs. Some powerful emotions broke loose inside of me then, and I lifted my face to meet the soothing jets of warmth: water and tears.

"Damn him!" I wailed, beating my fists against the slick squares of wet tile. "Damn him, damn the geese, damn becoming a woman, and damn *me* for trying so hard to be Mama. Damn every single, solitary thing in my life to Hell!"

At that moment, I was aware that, for better or worse, things were beginning to change inside me. Though I still loved and respected Pop and would never stop doing my best to keep the house and farm running smoothly, I knew that I would no longer be the compliant little girl I'd once been.

I used water that evening, lots of water—in fact, all the hot water. I didn't even worry about the drought. I didn't worry about Pop watering the garden. I didn't worry about our not having enough to wash with, or cook with, or drink. I just let gallon after gallon of that warm, soothing shower water pour down all over me, as comforting as Mama's hug and as melodious as her lullabies. And I felt my little-girl self slough off like old skin and wash clean and clear away.

Strides in the Snow

I WAS A GOOD GIRL, quiet, kind, and decent. I was hard-working and devoted to our farm and to my drawing projects. I tried my best to follow the rules and automatically obeyed people in charge. And in my world—the world of Plainfield, Missouri, in 1964—almost all those people were men, grown men, physically large, authoritative-acting adult males. As a small, thirteen-and-a-half-year-old girl who was barely five feet two in my stocking feet, I invariably deferred to them. Truth be told, I had always been more than a little intimidated by them.

My father—Pop—was by far the most important man in my life. He could do no wrong; his word was *law.* I loved him more than anyone and was eager to do whatever he asked. But I was also a little afraid of him. Since Mama's death, he'd become stern, and sometimes almost unapproachable. When he got upset, he was apt to be testy, and he couldn't stand what he called "damn foolishness." He would occasionally turn cold and barely talk to me, except for curt responses to my comments or questions. And he could be moody, disappearing into his own private world without warning and not coming out again for hours, even days. I wasn't always sure if he loved me—or if he even liked me all that much.

There was also Jared Tyler Morrison—Mr. M for short—who had taken me under his wing shortly after Mama died and was more of a friend and mentor than a true authority figure like Pop. He was patient and kind and seemed to understand me without my ever having to say a word. I admired him and visited him so frequently that his place became almost a second home to me.

And then there was Doc.

Doc Harris had been our family's physician since before Mama died. I was always polite and respectful in his presence, casting my eyes downward when speaking to him. But I didn't much like him. He was old and gruff and condescending. Whenever I visited him in his office, he'd pat me on the head as if I were still a little girl, and he'd tell jokes that weren't funny. Throughout my childhood, I'd had to put up with his behavior, but now, as a teenager, I felt that I'd do almost anything to avoid being around him.

Everyone in Plainfield knew Doc. Before retiring, he was the only physician in town who still made house calls. We'd see him speeding through town, white-knuckling the steering wheel with his eyes riveted on the road, on his way to deal with some medical emergency. He'd make calls at every hour of the day or night and in all types of weather. He was partial to Chevys. Fern green.

For years, he'd kept up his practice despite high blood pressure and a few minor strokes. But in his mid-seventies, he was forced to retire when doctors found blood clots in his legs, lying like torpedoes waiting to launch toward his heart or brain. If one of these clots broke loose, he'd be done for.

I knew nothing about any of this; and it probably wouldn't have lessened my dislike of the man anyway—a dislike that became even stronger one Saturday morning when Pop and I stopped, as was our weekly habit, at Roxanne's Diner for breakfast before shopping for groceries and picking up feed.

There, sitting in the main dining area of Roxanne's, was Doc, dressed in a suit, white shirt, and tie—same as he'd always worn beneath his lab coat when he saw patients in his office.

As luck would have it, he noticed me standing next to Pop at the cashier's counter. Though I tried to ignore him, he kept gesturing to me until I finally gave up and presented myself at the table where he was sitting with a group of his friends and his wife, Ruby Bea.

Aside from being ill-at-ease around Doc, I didn't trust him. Though I never blamed him for Mama's death, I couldn't get past what he did—or rather what he *didn't* do—back when I was eleven and Pop became so ill.

Doc had diagnosed Pop with walking pneumonia, but as it turned out that wasn't what afflicted my father at all. The medicine Doc prescribed offered little remedy; instead, Pop just kept getting sicker and weaker and thinner.

I'd hear him up nights, pacing the floor downstairs in the kitchen and coughing so hard I feared his insides would rip apart. Pop had suffered a separated rib from all that hacking, making it painful for him to do chores or much of anything else. I'd see him wince whenever he tried to lift things or accidentally turned the wrong way.

Soon I began to take over as many of the farm chores as I could manage. I was strong for my age, but I quickly grew weary from wrestling hay bales and hoisting sacks of feed. That, plus doing the cooking, cleaning, and laundry, worrying about Pop, and not getting much sleep, began to wear me down.

At night, I'd nod off while doing my homework and wake later to find my head cradled between the pages of an open book. Half-asleep and groggy, I'd stumble to my bed, claw my way under the covers, and doze until I heard Pop coughing. Then, I'd get up and go to him to try to help.

There wasn't much I could do for Pop—or much that he'd let me do. Just when he seemed to be hurting the most and I figured he'd welcome my help—or at least a little comfort and companionship—he'd withdraw into himself, saying he was all right and preferred to deal with things by himself.

His desire to be alone got worse after he became ill, but I'd go to him anyway. What seemed to work best was to boil water for tea, then add honey and lemon and whisky (not that I approved of liquor!) to make a toddy for Pop to sip between coughing spells. Sometimes I'd rub my hand up and down his back, hoping to soothe him. Mostly I prayed to God that he wouldn't die.

After a while, Pop would notice me sitting at the kitchen table, my forehead crinkled with worry. "You all right, Little Bit?" he'd ask.

"Yeah, Pop," I'd always say.

"Then you'd better go to bed, get some sleep."

I'd stay a couple of minutes longer—as long as Pop would let me—until he'd nudge my ankle with the toe of his work boot. "Bed," he'd repeat firmly.

"But you might need—" I'd start to protest, but Pop would take my arm, pull me onto my feet, and turn me in the direction of the stairs that led up to our bedrooms. "There's nothing you can do," he'd say. "I just have to ride this damn thing out."

I'd go back to bed but almost never fell asleep. Instead, I'd lie awake in the darkness, listening to him coughing and wishing I could do something to make him better.

Pop got so he looked awful. His complexion turned gray, and his weight dropped alarmingly, reminding me of how Mama looked in the months before she died.

One day in town, I overheard Ellen Lucas and Maudie French saying that Pop "looked like he had one foot in the grave" and "wouldn't it be a shame if he up and died and left that sweet little girl"—me—"an orphan." At odd times, their voices would come back to me, and tears would begin running down my cheeks before I could grab hold of my emotions.

Pop worried that he might have some strange form of TB and decided to find out. As if admitting defeat, Doc finally gave him the name of a specialist in Springfield, a hundred miles north of us. Pop phoned and set up an appointment. It turned out he'd developed something called histoplasmosis, a lung disease not unheard of in the farming country of north and central Missouri but fairly rare down in the rockier southern hills where we lived. Too bad it took three months to find out. By then, most of Pop's infection had run its course.

I had no interest in talking to Doc that Saturday morning at Roxanne's, but he was persistent. I walked over to him and said hello, trying my best to be polite. I was startled to see that he'd lost a lot of weight. His neck seemed to swim in his shirt collar. His hair was getting thin, too—just a few feathery gray wisps combed over the crown of his head. He asked where Pop and I had been keeping ourselves and said that life on our farm must be agreeing with us, since we hadn't been in to see him before he closed his office.

"We're okay," I mumbled.

He grunted an acknowledgement, then launched into a discussion of his youngest daughter, Marci, who was pregnant with her second child. He yanked my copper-colored braid, unloosing some of the curly strands that I always struggled to keep under control, and teased me, chuckling in a voice made rough by a half-century of pipe-smoking: "I'll bet you have lots of boyfriends. One of these years, you'll be starting a family, too!"

I was mortified to hear him talk about such things right out loud in public. My face burned red, especially when Doc's friends looked at me and snickered.

Ruby Bea, Doc's wife, didn't snicker. She arched her brows over her coffee mug and looked at me with an expression that seemed to say, "What's a person to *do* with someone like that?" I didn't know. Just endure, I guessed, which is what I did.

This was the first time I'd met Ruby Bea, and I was drawn to her right away. She cut a smart figure in a simple beige pantsuit accented with a blue paisley silk scarf knotted loosely around her neck. Though she'd been sipping coffee, her lips retained remnants of the rose-colored lipstick she'd put on that morning. Her face was round and smooth and framed by soft white curls, reminding me of the moon that I'd gazed at from my bedroom window almost every night of my life for as far back as I could remember.

As I looked at her sitting there next to Doc, creating an oasis of serenity amidst the hubbub of Roxanne's Diner, I longed to get to know her better. Having lost my mother when I was nine, I had no women in my life to advise me or to look up to as a role model. But how in the world would I ever get to know Ruby Bea Harris better? It certainly would never happen without my having to come into direct contact with Doc.

Pop walked over to the table, said a curt hello to Doc, and nodded to the others seated around him. Fortunately, he hadn't heard Doc's remarks. Pop could be prickly about personal matters.

The conversation was awkward. I knew Pop was anxious to leave and had better things to do than stand around shooting the breeze with Doc and his cronies. They traded a few more pleasantries, then Pop and I said our goodbyes and exited the diner.

It was odd, after that, how often I ran into Ruby Bea and Doc. Usually it was at Roxanne's when Pop and I stopped for breakfast. During those encounters, there was neither the time nor opportunity for any real interaction. As before, Doc'd see me and wave me over. I'd try to make small talk until Pop paid the check and signaled that it was time to go. Then, once outside, he'd complain that he didn't see why I always had to go over and talk to "that old quack."

"Well, what am I supposed to do?" I'd counter, feeling like Benedict Arnold for being unable to avoid such a situation. "Not go when Doc calls me over and cause a scene?"

"Humph," Pop would reply.

It was easier when I was alone. Walking home from school, I'd frequently see Doc and Ruby Bea around town doing errands. Doc wasn't allowed to drive anymore, so Ruby Bea—ten, maybe twelve, years younger than he was and in fine health—had to take him everywhere.

One afternoon, they invited me to their house. While walking home from school, I'd stopped at H. M. Farley's, a little mom-and-pop store that'd been in Plainfield for as long as anyone could remember, to buy milk and the daily newspaper, when I noticed them coming out of Doc's old office across the street. I walked over to them, and we began to talk. Soon it started to sprinkle. When the drizzle turned into a downpour, Ruby Bea suggested that we get into their car and finish our conversation at their place.

I called Pop from Doc's house and told him I'd be late. When he found out where I was, he had an edge to his voice that let me know I'd hear about it when I got home. But I didn't care. This was my God-given chance—maybe my one and only chance—to get to know Ruby Bea, and I wasn't about to let it pass me by. One visit led to another until soon it became a regular occurrence.

I loved talking with Ruby Bea. We'd discuss every topic under the sun—my dream of becoming an artist, the events in my life at home or school, and Ruby Bea's accounts of the goings-on around town and with her friends and children. When I spoke, her face would light up with almost maternal affection. She treated me with such kindness and understanding that I was pulled out of my innate shyness and talked freely about the daily concerns that confounded me—and especially why I felt so odd and different from everyone else around me.

Hearing this, Ruby Bea would chuckle and say, "But you're a teenager, my dear, and new to it, at that. You're no longer a child, but you're still not an adult. Nothing's the same; everything seems topsy-turvy. It's enough to make *anybody* feel peculiar."

Sometimes in our conversations, I'd complain about how Pop was so solemn and distant from me, yet, at the same time, overly protective. "Oh, honey," Ruby Bea would say. "I'm sure he means well. And I'm sure he loves you. Otherwise, why would he be so careful of you? He's just got a lot on his plate right now." She quickly glanced at Doc, who appeared to be dozing in his chair. She lowered her voice and said, "Besides, men are bossy. They like to be in control; they're born and bred to take charge. It's in their nature. You've just got to learn how to handle 'em." She glanced again at Doc before adding, "Take Doc and me. I give in to him most of the time—when it suits me, that is. But when he goes too far, I stand up to him and let him know it. As you get older and get more experience, you'll figure it all out."

"Hmmm," I thought. "I'm not so sure about that!"

Then something unexpected happened. The more I visited Ruby Bea and Doc, the more I began to see Doc as a real human being and not just a doctor. Before this, I'd believed that doctors were like the Almighty. After all, they had powers of life and death and knew things other people didn't. I thought physicians could work miracles. So when Doc didn't cure Pop—or accurately diagnose what ailed him—I damned him to Hell. It wasn't until after I started visiting Ruby Bea that I began to see Doc as a man who, like everybody else, had both good qualities and bad. Besides, Ruby Bea loved him and was making every effort to keep him interested in life. I found myself wanting to help, too.

If ever a man was unsettled, it was Doc after he was forced to retire. He'd expected to "meet his maker" while still practicing medicine—to die, in effect, with his boots on and perched high in the saddle, the way real men in westerns did. But his life didn't work out that way.

Over time my visits began to give Doc something to look forward to. They eased things for Ruby Bea, too. She said it got mighty quiet with "just the two of us sitting around staring at each other."

Once, after Doc had left the room, I pressed Ruby Bea to elaborate. "He doesn't have much to do anymore," she confided. "And nothing will ever mean as much to him as practicing medicine." She sighed. "He misses seeing patients and knowing he's making a difference—though, God knows, he kept going as long as he was physically able—maybe too long."

"What do you mean?"

"Do you remember when it was announced that the new hospital wing would be named in his honor?"

"Yes."

"Well, about the same time, Doc was voted off the board of directors of Plainfield Memorial."

The old man had served on the board since its inception, but in the latest election he'd been voted off by a group of younger doctors who'd risen to power—ones who'd had disagreements with Doc in recent years, calling his practices outdated. The young doctors felt justified in removing Doc because he was now retired from private practice.

As Ruby Bea related the chain of events, she blazed with anger. "Sure he's made mistakes. But who hasn't? It seems they could have done *something*—created some sort of honorary position on the board—and not just let the man feel like he's being totally put out to pasture!" she fumed. "Good grief! He was the first doctor to come to Plainfield and one of the founders of the hospital!" She fell silent as she struggled to regain her composure, then remarked testily, "Well, at least they *are* planning to name the new wing after him. That's *some* compensation."

"It's not fair!" I burst out. "After all he's done!"

"No, it's not fair," Ruby Bea agreed. "He tries not to show how deeply it hurt him, but I can tell it still cuts him to the quick. After all those years of service, to have no one appreciate him or call on him for advice anymore."

"I wish there was something I could do."

"Just keep coming by," Ruby Bea said. "He looks forward to your visits. They always cheer him up."

I watched as Doc walked back into the room and reseated himself. He moved more slowly than I'd previously noticed and seemed more uncertain when doing routine functions like lighting his pipe. In fact, at one point during my visit, he dropped his box of matches—the contents of which scattered like miniature pick-up-sticks on the floor next to his chair.

In a flash, I was off the sofa, stooping to retrieve the matches and replace them in their box before Doc could bend down to get them. When I handed Doc the box, I could see a look of anguish in his eyes. "Here, Doc," I said. "I think you're going to need these."

During my visits, Doc would sit in his recliner next to a lamp and smoking stand, dressed in his suit and tie, never saying much. But I'd see his expression brighten as soon as I stepped through the doorway and greeted him. He would sit listening to the murmur of Ruby Bea's and my voices as we talked, drawing methodically on his pipe—an ancient straight-shafted thing—which seemed at regular intervals to go out and have to be re-lit.

Periodically, our conversation would be interrupted by the ppfffhhh! of a lit match or the sharp, rhythmic staccato of Doc's knocking out the pipe bowl against the edge of the large glass ashtray on top of the stand. Half the ashes would land on the floor, where Caroline, the Harrises' pug-nosed dog, would try to lick them up before Ruby Bea could shoo her away. "Oh, Robert," Ruby Bea would sigh. Unconcerned, Doc would pull out a tin of Prince Albert and repack his pipe for a fresh smoke.

I loved the smell of the smoke. It reminded me of when Mama was still alive and Pop would relax with a pipe similar to Doc's. He'd hold me on his lap, and we'd become enveloped in a private smoky little cloud. I'd lean my head against his flannel shirt and hear his heart beating so strong and steady that I'd feel quiet inside, deeply comforted.

I imagined Doc's heart beating like that while he smoked. Sometimes he'd give me an empty tobacco tin with a trace of Prince Albert left in the bottom. The smell was reassuring—a reminder of Doc sitting in his chair puffing serenely while Ruby Bea and I held our regular weekly heart-to-hearts.

And speaking of regular, come four o'clock or so—as if set by some inner alarm clock—Doc would announce in his gravelly voice, "Time to go to Roxanne's." It didn't matter if Ruby Bea and I were deep in conversation; we had to stop talking and prepare to depart. Otherwise, Doc would sit in his chair, bang his pipe, glare at us, and harrumph.

Roxanne's was a lively place when it filled up: the best place in town for a bottomless cup of coffee, good food, and gathering with friends. It was a real meeting place for "regulars" like Doc.

Every morning at eight-thirty, maybe nine, and every afternoon around four-thirty, Doc and his friends would gather at Roxanne's to sip coffee and exchange views about the goings-on in the world, starting with general comments about the day's weather and progressing to quick snippets of information about family members before launching into a discussion of the cockamamie ways some officials in the town, the state, and beyond were running things. From locals like Mayor Doug Jones, or Ralph Reynolds, the president of the First National Bank, or Sam Moss, the editor of *The Plainfield Journal*, to Senator Neil Riley, Governor Mick Morris, or LBJ himself—no one escaped their scrutiny. Doc relished these times at Roxanne's. In truth, once he retired, he probably lived for them. He kept to his routine, no matter what—as I would find out one winter afternoon.

It was a Monday. After school every Monday I would stop by Doc and Ruby Bea's for my weekly visit. That worked out well, because I didn't have to tell Pop where I was going. Not that he would have been able to stop me, but he might have tried. At any rate, we would have argued ferociously. We did anyway when school let out for the summer and I wanted to continue my visits.

Pop was furious when I told him where I'd been spending my Monday afternoons. He'd assumed I was still at school, and called me a "deceitful little brat"—the most horrible thing he'd ever said to me in my life. He said I'd betrayed his trust, then muttered something about "was this how I showed my gratitude."

I couldn't understand why he was so upset. When I tried to find out, he snapped, "Never mind. You wouldn't understand!" and strode into the living room to stare out the window.

"What?" I asked myself. "*What* don't I understand?" I trailed after Pop to try to coax out an answer.

He turned and glared at me. "I shouldn't have to explain," he blustered. I stood my ground, looking back at him. Though clearly irate, he pulled himself together enough for a civil exchange. "I am your *father*, Hallie. It's my job to make sure you don't get hurt." I nodded, although to me *hurt* meant being kidnapped or molested by rednecks—or worse. He went on. "How can I *do* that when I don't know where you are?"

"But I *told* you!"

Pop raised an eyebrow. "Really? When?"

"Lots of times," I said evasively. "I know I mentioned it to you."

"And did I ever give you my consent?"

"I thought you did." Any trace of my bravura disappeared into the warm summer air. Pop had me. We both knew he had me.

"I most certainly did not!" His stare immobilized me. I kept quiet and let him continue. "I barely *know* those people."

"Yes, you do," I interjected as diplomatically as possible. "You've seen both of them at Roxanne's. And Doc's always been our doctor."

"That doesn't mean that I know them *personally*—or know you'd be safe with them."

"But they're nice people, Pop! Sort of like grandparents, only not as old. I love visiting them."

I could tell that my father was considering what I'd said and gave him all the time he needed. "That may be well and good," he conceded, "but I have to know where you are. And what time you'll be home."

"Well then, when do you want me home?"

"Four thirty, no later than quarter to five."

These conditions sounded more than fair, since that was about the time I'd been getting home anyway. "Okay, Pop," I said. "Then you'll let me go?"

"I suppose."

"Thanks, Pop." I felt light inside and happy enough to sing. On my way out of the room, I turned and said, "Pop, I'm really sorry."

I didn't talk much about my visits after that, but I still went. And I made double-sure I was home on time.

The weeks ran into months and the months stretched into a year.

One particular Monday afternoon, it was snowing to beat the band. There'd been no school, so I'd stayed home all day. At first, Pop wasn't about to let me out of the house. "Too dangerous in this weather," he insisted. We argued, but I was stubborn. I wanted to talk to Ruby Bea and absorb some more of my friend's warmth and wisdom. Besides, I knew Doc would be disappointed if I didn't come. I'd visited them every week for a solid year and wanted to prove to everyone that I wasn't some weakling who could be stopped by a silly old snowstorm.

I couldn't tell Pop all this. He never would have understood. In fact, when I first mentioned going, he got huffy and demanded, "Why're you always running off to visit that old man? I don't know what you see in him."

My face flushed before I could gather myself to reply, "What do you mean 'see that old man'? Doc's sick. Isn't it our Christian duty to cheer up the sick?" Since Pop was the pastor of a small local church, I was certain that this line of reasoning would persuade him.

Pop muttered something I couldn't understand.

"Besides," I continued, "I don't talk to Doc much. Mostly it's just Ruby Bea and me. We talk about women things— stuff *you* wouldn't know anything about!" That last part came out snippier than I'd intended, but I held my ground.

Pop gave me a sharp look.

It took longer than usual to make my way down off the ridge that led from our farm to Doc's house in town. I had to wear my tall rubber farm boots to plow a path through snow that, in spots, reached almost to my knees and was coming down so thick it nearly covered me. I could barely see my way and had to trudge slowly to keep from stumbling and rolling down the slope. But Doc was counting on me to come. I had to. I'd become part of his routine.

When I arrived, I saw him settle into his chair with a nod and a satisfied smile. Ruby Bea fussed and clucked while she dusted me off on the back porch, saying she really hadn't expected me to come that afternoon on account of the storm.

I noticed that her voice sounded husky. "Sore throat," she explained. "Woke up with it this morning. Don't know *how* I ever got it; I hardly ever get sick." We went inside and settled on the sofa to talk, with no inkling about what Doc might soon have in mind.

But a little before four o'clock, his voice rasped into our conversation. "Time to go to Roxanne's."

It took a second or two for his words to register. I was startled, but Ruby Bea rose to the occasion. "And just how do you intend to get there, Robert?" she inquired. "Surely, you don't expect *me* to take the car out in weather like this. The streets are completely covered. No one's out on the road. It's impossible to drive."

"Then I'll walk," Doc replied, with a stubborn set to his jaw.

The notion was almost laughable. With three clots in his legs, it was hard enough for him to hobble around with a cane in clear weather, much less try to push through a foot and a half of wet, heavy snow with more coming down by the minute. His doctors were concerned about the clots breaking loose and entering his blood stream, and he was taking medication to try to dissolve them. It was the mid-sixties and medical science wasn't yet advanced enough for them to be removed surgically. His left leg was especially vulnerable. If the medication didn't work, the leg might have to be amputated. It followed, without saying, that Doc wasn't supposed to over-exert himself.

Ruby Bea and I looked at each other, our eyes locked in silent communication. "Is he serious?" I asked, raising my eyebrows. "Completely," Ruby Bea nodded, with a grim smile.

"I'll walk," Doc repeated, and Ruby Bea and I knew we had a fight on our hands. Whenever Doc decided to do something, he'd do it or practically die trying. Ruby Bea began to argue with him; for the time being, I kept quiet.

"You are *not* going to walk to Roxanne's or anyplace else," Ruby Bea replied.

Doc fiddled with his pipe, ignoring her.

Ruby Bea continued, her voice rising. "Are you out of your *mind*? Don't you see how hard it's snowing? And have you forgotten your *legs*? You know *well and good* you have no business walking that far." Doc kept fiddling with his pipe while Ruby Bea forged ahead. "All you need to do is break one of those blood clots loose, and you've had it! Think, Robert! Do you want to drop dead out there on the street?"

"*I . . . am . . . going . . . to . . . walk . . . to . . . Roxanne's,*" Doc announced, looking combatively at his wife.

"Robert, I simply can't put up with your childishness!" Ruby Bea looked as if she wanted to shake Doc or pick up the needlework she'd been working on and hit him over the head with it.

"Come on, Doc," I pleaded. "Can't you wait until tomorrow? The snowplow will have come through by then, and the roads will be clear enough so Ruby Bea can drive you. You don't have to go there today. Everybody'll understand. It's terrible outside! There's snow clear to my knees and more's coming down. Must be close to two feet by now. I could barely make it through."

Oh, dear. As soon as the words left my mouth, I wished I could take them back. Doc glared at me. I could read the message in his eyes: "If some runt of a girl like you can get through that snow, then so can I!"

"Uh-oh," I thought. "We're dealing with masculine pride and a test of manhood here. The old man would rather die than be outdone by a girl!" I resented Doc for being so . . . so male and so completely unreasonable. "Damn it, Doc!" I shouted.

"Don't curse," he snapped.

I tempered my words. "But Doc, you *can't* go; you just *can't!*"

Truth be told, I understood his pugnacious attitude. But I didn't dare let on. I decided I'd best let Ruby Bea handle the situation.

"Robert! Robert!" Ruby Bea called out in a last-ditch effort to stop her husband, who had begun, slowly but deliberately, to limp out of the room. He just kept walking and didn't pause or look back. "I give up! I absolutely *give up!*" Ruby Bea's voice cracked before she succumbed to a prolonged fit of coughing. When she recovered, she said grimly, "Okay, then, go. Go! If you choose to go out in this weather and risk your life, I can't stop you. You're a grown man, Robert. Do what you please."

She said this, but I knew that she was scared to death. I knew, too, that she might risk catching pneumonia if she tried to walk the mile or so to Roxanne's with her husband.

Doc made his way to the hall closet, hauled out a pair of tall, old-fashion zip-up rubber boots, and put them on unzipped, followed by his overcoat. Then, with boots flopping, he walked down the hallway toward the front door.

"Good grief, Doc! At least let me zip your boots up!" I yelled after him. I glanced at Ruby Bea, who looked crumpled. I longed to ease her burden—to soothe the woman who had soothed me so many times in the past year. But I also felt strangely moved to help Doc to do what he seemed so compelled to do. "But you can't go out alone. Come on back, Doc," I said. "If you'll just wait a minute, I'll go with you."

We waded out into the driving snow: two dark figures in high boots and heavy coats in a world of white. The sidewalks and streets had disappeared. The plow hadn't come through yet, and no one was about to shovel their walks until the snow let up.

It didn't take long for me to realize that Doc wasn't going to make it very far, stumbling along with only a cane for support. I'd never seen him look so frail and uncertain. He seemed subdued, too—as if he'd just realized the full scope of what he was attempting to do. I hooked my arm through his to help him along. He kept looking ahead but gave my arm a squeeze. Meanwhile, I was beginning to think all this had been a hideous mistake and wondered if, come the spring thaw, Sheriff Dixon would discover our frozen-stiff bodies in a melting snowbank.

I began a running commentary about the particulars of the sidewalk, so Doc wouldn't stumble and fall. "Sidewalk's ending now. Step down," I'd say. Or, "Now here's the sidewalk, again. Step up."

It was slow and strenuous business. I began to worry, "His legs! His heart! His lungs! This is going to kill him!"

Soon, however, Doc seemed to gain more confidence. After eight blocks, his eyes lit up and his lips began to widen with a hint of a satisfied smile—or at least as much of a smile as a mouth can have with an unlit pipe clenched between its teeth.

"Good God!" I said to myself. "He's actually enjoying this! He's having the time of his life!"

"Fun, huh?" Doc rumbled.

As we plowed on, people peered at us from behind their curtains. A couple of pickups crawled by, the drivers doing a double-take at the sight of us plodding along. "To Hell with them," I muttered to myself. "And to Hell with Doc and Roxanne's. In fact, to Hell with this whole damned business."

Except, in an odd way, I was starting to enjoy the insanity of our situation and to feel a kind of camaraderie with Doc— the last thing in the world I ever expected would happen with the man who'd once caused Pop and me so much grief.

Suddenly Doc's cane skittered and he went down, taking me with him with nothing more than a bank of snow to cushion our falls.

I was terrified to look at Doc, but there he was, lying on his side, immobile. His eyes were shut. Was he unconscious? Dead? Oh why oh why had I *ever* offered to help him get to the diner?

Doc groaned and opened his eyes.

"You okay?" I quavered.

"Think so," Doc said.

"Thank God," I said under my breath, then asked him, "Did you hit your head? Do you have any broken bones?"

"Don't think so." Doc groaned again and rolled onto his back. And there he stayed without moving a muscle.

Meanwhile, I was doing my level best to stay composed and clear-headed. Though I felt shaky inside, I didn't dare give in to tears; they wouldn't help anything. One thing I knew for sure: I needed to get Doc up and out of the snow and to safety, as quickly as possible.

About then I heard an odd sound—something that sounded like the wheezing of a rickety old engine. "Heh!" it went. "Heh-heh! . . . Heh-heh-heh!" I looked at Doc. Why, the old man was flat on his back and laughing!

And he was moving his arms up and down and scissoring his legs as he lay prostrate on the sidewalk in front of the Hendersons' house on Main Street.

"My God, Doc!" I cried. "What are you *doing*? That fall could've killed you—and now you're making snow angels and laughing like a fool!"

"Wouldn't be the first time," Doc chortled.

"I'm dealing with a madman," I said under my breath. "God Almighty, Doc! You could have been *killed*!"

"But I wasn't, was I?"

"But you might've . . . ."

"So what?"

"What do you mean, 'so what'? You could be dead right now right out here in the middle of the sidewalk."

"Hell, I'm a tough old bird," Doc replied. "I've been through worse than this, and I'm still alive." I looked at him and grunted. "And so what if I'd died?" he added.

"So *what*?" I almost choked.

Doc went on. "Better to die out here than sit around the house worrying about things I really can't change and dying a slow death anyway. Sometimes it's better to stare death in the face and spit at it rather than sit around waiting for it to come—and it *will* come."

"But Doc!"

"But nothing!" the old man shot back. "I'm okay, and so are you. We may be stove up—really sore with a bruise or two—for a couple of days, but who cares? It was worth it." He shifted back onto his side. "Now help me up, unless you want us to lie here for the rest of the afternoon, freezing our tails off and scandalizing the passers-by—as fun as that might be."

Fun? This was hardly my idea of fun. I began thinking about what I needed to do to get us out of this mess. Then I knew. Directly, I rolled onto my hands and knees and scrunched them firmly into the snow. I told Doc to roll onto *his* hands and knees and drape himself over my back. It took some time and effort, but he did it. Then, I took a deep breath and began to push up onto my feet with Doc leaning onto my back until he regained his footing.

"Hold steady, Doc," I huffed, "while I grab your cane."

"And don't forget my pipe. . . ."

We brushed ourselves off and continued ahead, finally making it to an imposing Victorian residence several blocks from the diner. A gazebo offered some welcome shelter. Doc's breathing seemed labored, so I suggested we stop. Without comment, Doc took cover, then knocked out his pipe, took out his Prince Albert, and began to repack it for a smoke.

By now, the snow was beginning to let up, but it had taken us nearly an hour to trudge three-quarters of a mile. Of course, it was a minor miracle that Doc had made it this far, especially after his fall.

He tried to light his pipe several times, but the matches kept blowing out. I tried to help by cupping my hands around the bowl, but even that didn't work. But Doc didn't seem perturbed. He just held the unlit stem in his mouth, leaned against the gazebo, and calmly contemplated the snow.

Suddenly, the full impact of Doc's fall hit me, and I muttered, "God, Doc, if anything had happened to you, I'd never, ever forgive myself! And Ruby Bea wouldn't forgive me, either. She'd never speak to me again!"

"You'd be surprised."

I looked at him quizzically.

"Don't you think that after forty-some years of marriage my wife knows what makes me tick? And knows what I want and need to do?"

"But you might have died!"

"I might have, but I didn't," Doc responded, "thanks to your good judgment and quick thinking, getting me back on my feet like that. You've got a good head on your shoulders, young lady. Pretty impressive."

Doc finally got his pipe lit and leaned back against the wall of the gazebo. And not a thing in the world could wipe the smile off his face. "We're having us quite an adventure this afternoon. Thank you for coming out with me." He took a couple of puffs on his pipe.

When Doc's breathing had steadied, we started again. It took another fifteen minutes to reach Roxanne's, and, sure enough, most of Doc's friends had already made it in.

The minute he stepped through the door, he was greeted by Ross Malone's voice, rising above the clatter of the diner, "Well, I'll be *damned*! Look who's here!"

"Jesus, Doc! You walked all this way?" said Vernon Clark, amazed to see the old man standing before him in the flesh.

How they ooo-ed and ah-ed over the fact that he'd managed to get there—on foot, no less!—in the heaviest snow storm of the winter. There were backwards and forwards comments ending with someone saying, "Better take a load off and get yourself a cup of coffee."

Doc took his place at the table among his friends, thoroughly enjoying all the fuss being made over him. It was exactly what he'd seemed to need: proof to his wife, to me, to his cohorts, and to the whole damned world, that he was still a capable man—one strong and smart and stubborn enough to handle any challenges that life threw at him.

The remarks from the regulars continued. "You mean Ruby actually *let* you come out in all this?" Ron Jessup piped up.

Doc raised and lowered his eyebrows. "Not exactly . . . ."

"Bet she really pitched a fit." Grand Hardy ventured.

"She did," Doc acknowledged.

"And for good reason," I thought but didn't say aloud.

"Anyway, it didn't work," Doc added, drawing deeply on his pipe.

"Well, a man's gotta do what a man's gotta do," the group concluded.

Inwardly, I sighed. "And what's a *woman* gotta do? Keep her mouth shut while her man bull-headedly marches off into danger?" I looked at the regulars, now sipping coffee and talking together as if I didn't even exist; it was man's-talk in a man's world.

About then I noticed the time. It was a good hour later than when I was supposed to have been home. A sense of doom descended upon me. "Pop is going to kill me!" I thought. I knew I'd better call him before he phoned Ruby Bea or, worse yet, came out looking for me.

When Pop picked up the receiver, he was almost too angry to speak. I assured him I'd be home within the half-hour. After making sure someone would give Doc a ride home, I said goodbye to him and his friends, now settling into a debate about how long the winter was going to last and who would be the last person in town to shovel their sidewalks. As I headed out the door, Doc nodded at me, smiled, and saluted.

As difficult as it was, I slogged the mile or so up the side of the ridge to our farm. It was now almost dark and way past the time I'd promised to be home.

As I made my way back, I planned a counterattack to what I knew would be Pop's fury about my being so late. For one thing, I decided that before he had a chance to say anything, I'd start telling him what had happened with Doc, emphasizing that Ruby Bea was sick and needed help.

Pop was standing at the door and looking as huge and mean and enraged as the black bull my brothers used to tease when I was a little girl. He seemed bigger and taller than I'd ever seen him—so tall that all I noticed was his large, worn silver belt buckle imprinted with his initials. His hands, each looking as big as my head, hung at his sides, flexing and un-flexing in an agitated state.

"Now he really doesn't love me any more," I thought. "And he's so angry he's really going to let me have it."

I looked up at him. The expression on his face was so dark and terrible that my knees almost buckled. His face was red, and his eyes, glowing with rage. I looked down again and saw one of his hands close into a fist and start to come up.

"Damnation!" he shouted as he struck the doorjamb above my head. "Hellfire and damnation!"

I was taken aback. Though Pop was an ordained minister, he'd always made liberal use of "damn" to emphasize his points. But his invocation of "hellfire and damnation" outside the confines of a sermon meant he'd been pushed to the limit. *I* had pushed him to the limit.

Without another word, he turned and stomped away.

"Wait, Pop!" I pleaded. "Don't go! Not now! Please just *listen* to me."

He spun around, strode back, and grabbed me by my shoulders. "Don't you *ever*—" he began, punctuating each word with a not-so-gentle shake.

"Wait!" I summoned all my courage, took a deep breath, and said in as firm and mature a voice as I could manage, "I think it's only fair that you let me explain!"

"Are you calling me unfair, young lady?" Pop fumed, giving my shoulders a final shake.

"No, of course not!" I stepped away from him.

"Do you know how *worried* . . . ?" he sputtered. "Why, I almost . . ."

"I know, Pop. I know. And I'm really sorry. It'll never happen again. But Pop, just listen to me for a minute!" I grabbed his arm and made him sit on the sofa. Then I stood in front of him, took another deep breath, and began relating what had happened. For the most part, Pop just glared.

After recounting my adventures and explaining Doc's determination to get to the diner, I asked him point-blank, "What would *you* have done?"

He thought for a minute. "Damned if I know!" he conceded. "I suppose I'd have done the same damn-fool thing!"

Before he could collect himself and return to the offensive, I left the room to fix supper.

That evening, as I stood at the sink doing the dishes, I gazed out the kitchen window at my old friend the moon and replayed the events of the day in my mind. It had been an extraordinary day, unlike any I'd ever experienced. I'd stood up to Pop for the first time in my life and, somehow, had managed to get away with it! In fact, Pop had listened to me and even intimated that my behavior with Doc that afternoon had been mature and responsible.

Yes, I thought to myself, I really had acted grown up—stepping in to help when Doc had insisted on walking to Roxanne's, then taking charge when he fell and I had to get him back on his feet and the rest of the way to the diner. Doc had appreciated my help and treated me like an adult. He had complimented my good judgment.

It had all been interesting—and very enlightening. Maybe all these male authority figures in my life weren't quite so intimidating after all.

The Will of God

I REALLY THOUGHT I WAS MAKING PROGRESS. It had been five years since Mama's death, and the melancholy ache that had held me in its grip was gradually fading, just as my adult friends Ruby Bea Harris and Mr. M had told me it would. Life seemed almost manageable. Then, out of the blue, *it* happened.

I was sitting next to Ruby Bea in church that Sunday morning, feeling as content as a well-fed cat. On the Sundays when there was a guest preacher at Pop's church, Good Shepherd of the Ozarks, I'd sometimes attend Ruby Bea's church, the First United Methodist, in town. We'd just had the Offertory, and I felt proud to have given two dollars instead of my usual one. Then, as was the custom, members of the congregation rose to sing the Doxology. "Praise God from Whom All Blessings Flow" emanated from me in full and joyous voice.

I was full of the Spirit by the time the morning sermon began, one about resisting temptation. Reverend Mitchell began by summarizing the story of The Fall. According to the biblical account, God made Adam and Eve to be companions to each other and live forever in the Garden of Eden, a place providing an abundance of food to be had just for the picking.

They were, however, forbidden to eat fruit from the Tree of the Knowledge of Good and Evil—a lovely tree growing in the center of the Garden and laden with fruit. The fruit, traditionally said to be apples, was deemed poisonous—if they ate it, they would die.

One afternoon, according to the account, a serpent persuaded Eve to eat an apple from the tree, telling her that after doing so she would not die but would instead have as much knowledge as God. Adam ate some of the fruit, too. When God discovered they had disobeyed Him, He banished them from the Garden. As further punishment, He decreed that although Eve would find sexual relations pleasurable, she would endure great pain during childbirth. He also cursed the soil outside the Garden, so that Adam would have to work long and hard to grow food for his family's survival. And rather than live for eternity in Paradise, Adam and Eve and all their descendants would eventually die and be returned to the ground "from whence they had come." And so it had been ever since.

After finishing his version of "paradise lost," Reverend Mitchell discussed some current instances of temptation: drinking or eating to excess, using mind-altering drugs, pre-marital sex, lying, stealing, cheating, or short-changing people at work. "You sinners know who you are," he warned.

Suddenly my mind backtracked to Adam and Eve. I'd heard about "The Fall" and "original sin" many times before. The story was a favorite of the hard-core hellfire-and-damnation sects whose songs, sermons, and testimonies dominated the radio airwaves of our Ozark region every Sunday. The convictions powering their messages could be terrifying but also seductive. The "Pentecostal Hour of Power" was the most convincing of all the gospel programs. It aired on KRPZ, our local station in Plainfield, Missouri, after supper about the time I was washing the dishes.

The program always opened with Preacher Billy Ray Hutchins's effusive invitation for listeners to join him in praising the Lord, followed by a song that Billy Ray and his wife, Bobby Sue, would sing about the glory of living a God-filled life. Billy Ray would then turn to the topic of sin and sinners, condemning everyone from locals like old Gus Simons, the town drunk, and Charlie Anderson, the Plainfield lawyer who'd up and left his wife and family for parts unknown with a young female assistant, to prominent people in the world at large. Feminists and feminism were a particular abomination to him, as were current women's fashions—mini-skirts, shorts, sleeveless blouses, and tank tops—clothes that according to Billy Ray were so scandalous that anyone wearing them "might as well be nekkid." Women who wore pants of any sort were, in his view, equally guilty of sinfully immodest behavior. I hoped the hand-me-down overalls I wore on the farm didn't count.

Invariably, Preacher Hutchins would next urge listeners to give their lives to Christ and be reborn into a new, godlier life according to the Gospels. He'd summarize what men needed to do to be godly: honor God, avoid temptation, and uphold family values.

Frequently, he would also add a lengthy treatise on women's behavior. He'd remind everyone about Eve, who'd disobeyed God and introduced sin into the world. Because of this, women—all of Eve's female descendants—needed to be vigilant about their behavior and lead a pure and godly life according to the Holy Scriptures.

According to Billy Ray, women could be as cunning and seductive as the serpent in the Garden, serving as Satan's messengers tempting men to commit grievous sins. This, he said, was exactly what women's-rights advocates and other ungodly women were trying to do. The proper hierarchy in God's order of life was "God-Christ-Man-Woman-Child," and women must know their places. "Sisters, don't be taken in by such evil!" he'd admonish. "Watch yourselves! Mend your ways!" He'd sometimes get so wrapped up in his entreaties that he'd begin to speak in tongues, after which he'd end the program with a solemn rendition of "Rock of Ages."

Over time, some of those Pentecostal messages had apparently taken root inside me, because right in the middle of Reverend Mitchell's Methodist church service that Sunday morning, it hit me like a boot kick to the stomach that, just as Billy Ray Hutchins had said, Eve—the mother of all mortals, the very first female, a woman who probably hadn't been much older than my fourteen and a half years of age—had caused the downfall of humankind. Her sin was so egregious that it had affected every man and woman who'd walked the Earth ever since.

I stopped paying attention to the sermon and followed my thoughts. It was because of Eve's original sin that there was so much trouble and misery and death in the world. Didn't the Bible say so? Preacher Hutchins was adamant in his certainty of this. "Mama's death?" popped into my head, and I felt sick to my stomach.

Then another revelation hit me: Eve's gullibility had made her untrustworthy. She'd believed the words of a serpent and ignored the primary edict of God: that she and Adam were forbidden to eat fruit from the Tree of Knowledge. If she, the pristine first woman, could be persuaded to disobey the Almighty, then way less perfect females like me were even more susceptible to sin and needed to be watched carefully.

"Maybe this is why Pop's afraid to let me out of his sight," I thought to myself. "Maybe he's worried I'll commit some heinous sin that'll last forever." Though it was cool inside the church, I began to sweat.

Resting next to the hymnal in the holder in front of me was a Bible. I was reluctant to distract Ruby Bea but felt obliged to check some Scripture. "I need to look something up," I whispered as Ruby Bea looked at me, nodded, then smoothed her skirt and re-focused on the sermon. I opened the book to Genesis, where it was written: "If you eat of the fruit, you will be doomed to die." I kept on reading until I came to the command God had given to Eve: "Your husband will be your master."

So there it was, just as Billy Ray Hutchins had said.

But if Adam was Eve's master, then where did that put me? Surely, a father was just as important as a husband—maybe even more so. The commandment to "honor thy father and mother" reverberated inside my head, reminding me that God wanted me to revere—make that *obey*—Pop no matter what.

I recalled the times I'd sneaked off to visit Ruby Bea and her husband. Well, I hadn't exactly *sneaked* off, but sometimes I'd been vague about telling Pop where I was going. Had I ever lied to him? I didn't think so. But any sort of deception was dishonoring Pop, wasn't it? And this meant that I must be a genuine, grade A sinner.

I suddenly felt aflame with remorse. I was certain that I was bad, truly bad—wicked through and through—and the only thing I could think of to try to save myself was to dedicate myself to living a purer, godlier life.

The phrase "God's will" suddenly floated into my consciousness, and I shuddered. I'd heard people say this all my life, usually after some tragedy had struck. Though the words were meant to console, they'd always bothered me.

At Mama's funeral back in 1960, several of the most pious mourners had professed that her death was "God's will" and that "The Lord giveth, and the Lord taketh away."

I was just nine years old at the time, and those words derailed me. Did this mean that God had *wanted* Mama to die? That He'd sat up there in Heaven and actually *planned* for Mary Elizabeth Everheart, the loving wife of William and devoted mother of three children—my very own Mama!—to slowly and painfully be consumed by cancer? Now, what kind of a God was one who had a will like that?

It had taken a good week or so after Mama's funeral for me to gather enough courage to bring this matter up with Pop. Despite his pastoral training, he couldn't abide "damn foolishness," so I knew I'd better choose the right moment to approach him and plan beforehand exactly what I wanted to say.

Summoning up my courage, I marched out to the barn. The light inside it was dim, illuminated only by the open door and a few streaks of sunlight making their way through the unwashed windows and cracks in the walls. I sidled up to Pop, who was bent over, pouring out feed for our new shipment of Rhode Island Red chicks, then took a deep breath and blurted out, "Pop, did God want Mama to die?"

"What?" he said, looking up.

"Was it really God's will that Mama should die, like people said at the funeral?"

Pop straightened up and stared at me. "It was cancer!" he muttered. "Spread all through her body! Pure and simple!" He went back to filling the feeder, shaking his head. "I don't know where this girl gets such crazy ideas!"

That had settled my concerns for a while, but I always had a vague, lingering feeling in the back of my mind that maybe it really *had* been God's will that Mama had died. Maybe I'd done something wrong—hadn't been good or obedient enough—and He'd decided to punish me by taking Mama away. And if He'd punished me once, He could do it again—maybe even take Pop.

This was too terrible a matter to discuss with my father. What if he said yes? Then, I'd have to run off and never be found—or maybe even kill myself.

Now, five years later on that Sunday morning in the First United Methodist Church, another strategy crept into my mind: I would need to push out sin and learn God's will through prayer and sacrifice. "The Will of God" had forced its way back into my life again. No matter how much the phrase bothered me, I knew I needed to figure out what "His will" was for my life, and then do it.

Every morning and evening I prayed for enlightenment and guidance. I also began making sacrifices to God to atone for my sins. First, I gave up desserts. I'd known several girls at my junior high who'd given up ice cream or chocolate for Lent. I decided to go one step further and give up all sweets and desserts, forever.

I continued baking cookies and pies for Pop, so he wouldn't suffer. But I didn't eat them. Instead, I'd serve him his dessert, then go directly to the sink to wash the supper dishes.

My change of behavior puzzled Pop. "Aren't you going to have dessert?" he'd ask.

"Not tonight, Pop," I'd reply. "I have a lot of homework to do." This wasn't a total lie: all that Bible reading and praying *did* take up considerable extra time.

He'd stare at me and begin to probe. "Since when have you ever refused dessert?"

"Maybe I'll have some later," I'd say, knowing full well that this was about the last thing in the world I intended to do.

I soon began thinking up additional sacrifices that I could make. During his radio broadcasts on Sunday evening, Billy Ray Hutchins reminded his listeners that according to the Bible, the key to becoming worthy was self-denial. If he was correct, I realized that everything I enjoyed must be evil.

So I started to question everything that gave me pleasure or even the tiniest bit of satisfaction, reminding myself that following God's "True Path" wasn't supposed to be easy.

I thought long and hard about all the activities I loved best. Should I give up my weekly visits to my friends Ruby Bea and her husband? No, I decided. That would penalize *them*, because they always looked forward to my stopping by.

Should I stop seeing our close family friend Mr. M? That would be impossible because he and Pop got together so often.

Then it came to me: to become worthy, I needed to give up working on my art projects. By doing so, I would be making a true and worthy sacrifice—my greatest sacrifice—because drawing and painting were the activities I enjoyed more than anything else. They were part of my daily routine, a way of helping me make sense of the world. I sketched every day after school—and frequently *in* school, when I was supposed to be working on something else—drawing anything that caught my fancy, from household objects to the insects and flowers in our gardens, to our weathered outbuildings and barnyard animals. Now it was suddenly clear to me: if I was sincere about cleansing myself of sin, such activities were self-indulgent pleasures that had to be sacrificed.

So I put away my pads and pencils, my charcoals and crayons, my watercolors and inks.

Within a few weeks, however, I began to feel anxious and depressed. Without drawing, life seemed flat and empty. I didn't know how I could live without making my art. But I knew I had to try.

I also tried harder than ever to obey Pop without a single argument or question or even so much as a sour expression on my face.

Pop soon took notice and asked if I'd been taken ill.

I looked at him with what I imagined was a saintly expression on my face. "No, Father. I'm fine, just fine."

"Father?" His eyes bored into me with a look so intense that I felt like I was under a microscope. He shook his head, sighed, and walked away.

As I fell deeper and deeper into depression, I didn't eat or sleep much, and I found it increasingly difficult to concentrate on anything. As the weeks went by and I grew more and more gaunt and haggard-looking, Pop became concerned. "What's happening?" he asked. "Are you sick? Do I need to take you to a doctor?"

"I'm fine," I said.

"No, you're not fine," Pop shot back. "You're anything but fine. You're not eating, and it looks like you haven't slept in days. You walk around like you're in a daze, looking almost as miserable as when your mother died."

"Dear God," I thought. "Why does he have to bring Mama into this?" I still hadn't shaken the fear that somehow I'd been to blame for Mama's death, that God had decided to punish me because I was too unworthy.

Pop reached out and stroked my cheek. "I can't help you if you won't tell me what's wrong."

"I'm okay, Pop," I murmured. "I'm just feeling a little low. It'll pass . . . ."

The next day was Saturday, and Pop said he needed to drive over to Mr. M's place. In the pickup, my stomach began rumbling loudly and persistently with hunger pangs. Pop didn't say anything, but I could sense that he was worrying about me.

Pulling into Mr. M's gravel driveway, we were greeted by the usual rush of barking dogs with their tails wagging wildly. When I stepped out of the truck, I was immediately engulfed by them, and I felt a rush of joy—the first I had experienced in weeks. The dogs' exuberance was so infectious that it cut through my depression.

By this time, our friend had come out onto the porch. "They don't care a bit about you, Will!" he called out to my father.

"Howdy, Slim," Pop said.

Mr. M ushered Pop and me into the living room, which over the years had become as familiar to me as our own house. On the table next to the velvet-covered wing chair— as always—there was a sketchpad and pencil waiting for me. "I guess you know what to do," he said, and he and Pop left the room.

I sat back into the chair, feeling drained of all energy and fragile enough to shatter. I also felt guilty. I knew Mr. M expected me to pick up the sketchpad and begin drawing, same as always. But no matter how much I wanted to, I was convinced that the salvation of my soul and Pop's safety depended upon my ability to resist the temptation.

It was peaceful in the room. The only sounds were the tick-tock of the grandfather clock and the far-off sound of the men's voices. The combination was pleasant, like a low-pitched lullaby, and the contours of the chair held me warmly and protectively, inviting me to let go of my worries and rest.

As if in a dream, I suddenly saw a creature slip past the living room door. Had I really seen it, or was it just a figment of my imagination?

The animal returned to the doorway. It was the color of dark honey and walked haltingly as it entered the room. I sat still, watching it as if it were an apparition from some otherworldly place. But it was real: the scrawniest dog I'd ever seen. It hobbled across the room to my chair, where it sniffed at my work boots and sneezed. Then it raised its head and sniffed its way up the legs of my overalls.

Quite without warning, it laid its head in my lap. "I know how you feel," I murmured as I ran a hand over its body. It was a female with a ribcage so prominent it reminded me of the frame of a sailing ship.

The dog raised its head and looked into my eyes. A world of sadness and suffering was reflected in its gaze. But there also seemed to be an innate curiosity and openness. I looked back at the animal. And, though many dogs are not comfortable with such a direct gaze, this creature's did not waver. Neither did mine.

We remained in deep communion for several minutes. I smoothed her soft fur, and she sighed contentedly and licked my hand. Finally, no longer able to summon the strength to support herself, she slid to the floor and collapsed, her head resting on my boot tops. Plainly, this good dog was exhausted and emaciated, almost to the point of death.

The dog's concave midsection rose and fell in rhythmic breathing. Soon the rhythm of my breathing matched hers. I struggled to keep my eyelids open, but they continued to droop and finally closed.

Suddenly, I felt a hand on my shoulder. I fought my way out of sleep and looked up.

"I see you've found the dog," Mr. M remarked. "Or rather, she's found you. I've got to say the two of you look pretty comfortable together!"

He offered me a mug. "Your father said you've been under the weather. I thought you could use some tea. Chamomile. It'll cure what ails you—or at least it'll help." I took the mug and cupped it between my hands. A wave of warm steam moistened my face, and I inhaled a faintly floral scent that was immediately soothing.

The dog stirred and yawned, then stretched her legs straight out in front of herself before refolding them against her body and curling into a bony ball. "Where'd she come from?"

"Showed up a couple nights ago. The dogs were barking. When I opened the front door, she was on the doorstep."

"How'd she get there?"

"No idea. The poor thing was used up, as if she'd traveled quite a ways. The pads on her feet were worn bad. She still favors them when she walks. And as you can see, she hadn't had any food in a long time."

"She's so skinny!"

"Starved and, at first, awful skittish." Mr. M shook his head. "She must be one strong animal to have survived— though the jury's still out on that."

"What do you mean?"

"It'll take some doing to bring her all the way back."

"But she *will* survive, won't she?"

"She's got to *want* to survive." He looked hard at me.

I reached down to stroke the gaunt animal resting against me. "She's so beautiful. And there's something really special about her."

Mr. M looked contemplative. "Looks like you've already become attached to each other."

"I want her to want to live. She's *got* to live." I whimpered.

"I'd say she needs you," Mr. M said quietly. "And I've got a hunch you need her, too. The two of you look like two peas in a pod—skinny and worn down. The two of you belong together."

I smiled and bent down to stroke the slumbering creature's coat. Maybe Mr. M was right: maybe we did belong together. From the moment we'd met, the dog and I had seemed to form a bond.

But then I remembered how horrible a sinner I was. My hand stopped its petting, and I straightened back up in the chair. I wanted that dog more than anything in the world, but I knew I couldn't have her. I didn't deserve her. I bit my lip to keep from breaking into tears.

Noticing the abrupt change in my demeanor, Mr. M asked, "What's the matter?"

"I—I can't have this dog," I choked out. "I can't have anything. There's no way."

"Why not? The two of you look like you're meant to be together. It's almost as though the dog sought you out." As if to reinforce his words, the animal lifted its head from my boots and looked up at me, then put its head back down with a soft sigh.

That did it. Tears began to cascade from my eyes.

"Tell me what's been happening," my friend said quietly.

"I'm not good enough to have her," I mumbled.

"What do you mean 'not good enough'? You're plenty good enough! Besides, this dog *needs* you."

"But I'm too much of a sinner," I whimpered.

"*What?*"

I grabbed hold of myself enough to speak. "Well, first of all, there's the whole Adam and Eve story," I said, "with Eve eating the apple and causing the downfall of all mankind. Womankind, too, of course." I wiped at my tears and sniffled. Mr. M pulled a handkerchief from his back pocket and handed it to me; I dabbed at my eyes, then blew my nose. "I realized that since Eve was the cause of all the sin in the world, then from the moment I was born I was a sinner, too.

"Some say we're all sinners."

"But women and girls are worse!"

"Well, I don't know about that."

"We are! And since, right from the start, women and girls have been more sinful, it means we have to work harder to be worthy and sacrifice more to atone for our evil."

"So what'd you do?" Mr. M asked, looking perplexed.

"I decided to cut out everything in my life that gives me pleasure," I said. "I figured if something was enjoyable or was something I was tempted to do, then it must be evil—a test from God to see how committed I was to doing His will and how worthy I was of His salvation. I began by giving up desserts, but that was too easy a sacrifice to be worthy of God. So I decided to get serious and eliminate any worldly pleasures." I took a deep breath and let it out before admitting, "Even drawing and painting."

Mr. M murmured something inaudible.

"That's what gives me the most pleasure, so it's the biggest sacrifice," I explained. "I figured I *had* to give it up. God doesn't make salvation easy. Satan's always out there putting temptations in our path to do things that aren't part of God's plan. At least that's what Billy Ray Hutchins says."

"Billy Ray Hutchins?"

"He's the preacher on the 'Pentecostal Hour of Power.' I listen to it on the radio every Sunday while I'm doing the dishes."

"Hmmm. . . ."

"It made sense to me that the more I enjoyed something, the greater the sin and the better the sacrifice."

Unable to restrain himself any longer, Mr. M blurted out: "You mean you've actually stopped drawing?" I nodded. "But you can't *do* that!" he protested. "You've got real potential."

"But I love it too much!" I argued. "I spend too much time working on my pictures instead of praying. And I use it to take me out of myself and my problems rather than relying on God!" Mr. M looked so dumbfounded that I explained. "It's a sin to love to do anything as much as I do drawing. It takes me away from doing the will of the Lord."

I began to sob.

The dog roused herself. With a groan, she pushed herself onto her feet and pressed into me, nudging my arms with her muzzle. And then I began to wail—all-out, noisy, ragged sobs that released all the pain and guilt trapped inside me.

When I finally caught my breath I felt shivery. And I was so embarrassed by my outburst that I couldn't even look at my friend.

"Have some tea," Mr. M said, handing me the mug. "It'll calm you down." When he spoke again, it was with great gravity. "Look at me, Hallie. I want to tell you something I don't think you've seriously considered."

I raised my eyes. Rather than looking disgusted, he was smiling compassionately at me. "You're a good girl, Hallie. And you're just not old enough to be a bona fide sinner." I took a breath, ready to protest, but Mr. M held up a hand to quiet me. "Hear me out." He leaned forward in his chair. "Did you ever think that your skill at drawing might be a gift from God?"

"You've said something like that before," I mumbled.

"Yes, I have! And I wasn't saying it just to hear my gums flap or to make you feel good. Before now, I don't think you've understood what I was getting at. Why do you think I've been pushing you to draw? Did it ever occur to you that becoming the best artist you can become might be God's *real* 'will' for your life? Think about it. Why would the Almighty give you talent if He didn't mean for you to use it?"

I sat thinking about what Mr. M had said. "I've never thought about it that way," I admitted. "That drawing might be what I was *supposed* to do and not just something I did for my own selfish pleasure."

Mr. M smiled. "You know, I believe that doing the will of God can involve a whole lot of things that aren't mentioned very much in traditional religion. No offense to Preacher Hutchins, but I'll bet my life he never talks about such things in his radio broadcasts." I shook my head, and Mr. M continued, "I think sometimes people get the wrong idea about serving God. Like you, they become convinced that it means they have to do something totally against their real nature. But to deprive yourself of something really important to your well-being doesn't seem to me to be very—well, godly."

"So," I began hesitantly, "what you're saying is that my becoming an artist is a gift from God—God's will—and if I don't use that gift, then it could be a sin?"

Mr. M groaned. "I really don't buy into the whole idea of sin; it's been used to cause people a whole lot of fear and misery and guilt over the centuries." Then, with a mischievous glint in his eyes, he said, "But if it gets you back to drawing, then, yeah, *do* consider that not doing it is a sin."

Suddenly there was a lot to think about. And though I could feel my attitudes begin to shift, it would take time for me to completely purge myself of the crazy, harmful ideas that had taken root inside me. And in the meantime, there was this dog nestled against me. I reached down and ran my hands over her body. As I caressed the animal, her head sank deeper into my lap. "I think she really likes me," I said.

"Of course she does. And she probably needs you at least as much as you need her." Mr. M looked serious. "Tell you what. I'll let you have her on one condition. You've got to promise me you'll get back to your drawing."

I smiled and nodded.

"And one more thing. You've got to tell your father everything you've told me."

About that time, the dogs in the yard began to bark, signaling Pop's return. A minute later, he appeared in the living room doorway. "Well, what do we have here?"

"Spirit!" I shouted, burying my face in the dog's fur.

"So, you've already named her," Pop remarked. And I had. Her name had come to me then and there on the spot.

Lowering his voice, Mr. M told Pop, "The kid's been dealing with some serious stuff. Seems she'd gotten some misguided—and real self-destructive—ideas into her head."

"I've been worried," Pop sighed. "But she wouldn't tell me a thing."

"Well, she never would've said anything to me, if it hadn't of been for the dog. But Hallie's promised to tell you everything."

That evening—as soon as I'd done the dishes—I talked with Pop. Every so often, he'd interrupt, expressing dismay about my suffering along with his outrage that I could have interpreted the Scriptures in such a skewed manner.

"I've never really believed all that stuff about Eve," he said, "though some preachers seem dead-set on blaming women for everything that's bad in the world to keep them quiet and obedient and in their places—like servants." He shook his head. "And they always come up with biblical references to 'prove' their claims! Understand, I'm not knocking the beliefs of any particular denomination. I just don't agree with some of them. And, fact is, a person can find passages in the Bible to back up just about anything. Personally, I've always liked a woman with a mind of her own—a woman who isn't afraid to use her brains and speak her mind. Your mother was like that. I counted on it and wanted her opinions." He paused, then said, "You're sort of like that, too.

"And as for the business about the Garden of Eden, you need to read the *King James* version. Then show me where it says that God spoke *directly* to Eve to tell her not to eat the fruit from that tree. I think you'll find that God spoke only to Adam about the apple, not Eve."

"What?"

He nodded. "I'm afraid traditional interpretations of The Fall sometimes leave out important details from the actual account in the Bible—maybe to shift some of the blame off Adam and his male descendants. We've been told that Adam was formed by God from the dust of the earth. He then told Adam—and *only* Adam—that he could eat anything in the Garden except for the fruit of the Tree of Knowledge. Shortly thereafter, He put Adam into a deep sleep and removed one of his ribs, from which He is said to have formed Eve. This means that Eve never heard the actual voice of God saying she was forbidden to eat the apple; she got that warning second-hand from her husband, who, at the time, had not been decreed as her 'master,' so she regarded him as her equal.

"When the serpent appeared to Eve and told her that eating the apple would give her as much knowledge as God, she was tempted. She was new to the world and eager to know everything she could about it and share it with her husband. Wouldn't you? And then Adam ate the fruit, too, and when God confronted him, he blamed his behavior on Eve! He said that she had given him the apple, and he'd eaten it. Some accounts soften Adam's offense by saying that he ate the fruit out of love for Eve, since he didn't want her to suffer God's wrath alone. But no matter how you cut it, it was *Adam* who directly disobeyed God. And no one put a gun to his head to force him to do what he knew was wrong. I guess he must have loved Eve more than God!" There was a trace of amusement in his voice. "To tell the truth, that last bit comes from your mother."

"Mama said all that?"

"You'd be surprised by the conversations your mother and I had. She was one of the most intelligent women I've ever met—and a godly woman fully versed in the Bible—but she had definite ideas and opinions about things and wasn't shy about expressing them. And don't ever get her riled!"

"Like about blaming everything on Eve?"

"That, and other things. She always maintained that we shouldn't condemn Eve but that instead we ought to celebrate her for having the courage to break the rules to try to gain more knowledge."

"I've never heard you talk like that about Mama or about religion."

"Look, Hallie, there's enough real evil in the world—and enough serious mistakes we all make—without adding the alleged sins of Eve and every other woman into the mix." He paused. "Here's something you need to consider: Christianity was founded on the belief that Christ sacrificed his life to atone for our sins. That means you don't have to sacrifice yours."

I was quiet while I tried to absorb what Pop was saying—so radically different from what I'd heard on the Sunday radio broadcasts.

"The next time you have questions about any of this stuff, for God's sake, let's talk about it. We've had our disagreements, but I can't think of a single thing you'd ever say or do to make me so upset that I wouldn't be proud you're my daughter. You're turning into a fine young woman, Hallie—one your mother would be proud of, too."

That night I unpacked my pads and pencils, my crayons, watercolors, charcoals, and inks and began drawing again.

The following Sunday, Pop and I brought Spirit home. My feelings of sinfulness and guilt were beginning to fade, like a bad dream.

After supper, I followed my normal routine by turning on the radio before I began washing the dishes. The familiar voice of Billy Ray Hutchins soon filled the kitchen with prophecies of salvation for those who walked the straight and narrow and eternal damnation for those who didn't. When he launched into his weekly condemnation of women, I reached for the dish towel, dried my hands, and switched off the radio. I had better things to think about.

New Clothes

HEY WERE OUT THERE: the cute girls, the popular girls, the upper-class girls who lived in town and came from money. They acted as if they owned our school. They certainly ruled it. Whenever one of them showed up with new clothes, new shoes, or a different hairstyle, the popular-girl-wannabes—and there were plenty of them at Plainfield High—fell all over themselves to buy into the latest trends.

It was 1966, and the British Invasion had hit our small Ozarks town. The popular girls had quickly perfected the mod Carnaby Street look, wearing skirts and dresses as mini as our school officials would allow and shiny white Mary Quant boots or Capezio ghillies in red, black, or navy. Their hair was flawlessly straight—long, like the model Pattie Boyd's, or short, like Twiggy's—with bangs that merged with their eyebrows to accentuate their eyes, meticulously made up with mascara, shadow, and liner to look large and mysterious. Rumor had it that some of the girls ironed their hair to get The Look.

I, Hallie Jo Everheart, hoped their hair would scorch, and maybe even ignite.

But there they were: the all-too-familiar cluster of them, looking me up and down with eyebrows arched and mouths twisted with scorn as I exited the girls' bathroom.

"Look at her," Mary Ann Jelks began, her voice dripping with disdain. "She's so *odd*. So *out-of-it*."

"Doesn't she even *know*?" Fran, her twin sister, piped up.

"Hardly," Lynnette Gregg drawled. "All that girl ever thinks about is drawing."

"So what?" I thought as I pushed forward, trying my best to ignore them.

They were more vicious than last year. Freshmen were considered hopeless—beneath the group's contempt—but sophomores like me had better shape up and fit in, or else.

Their assault on me ramped up, their voices so penetrating that I was sure everyone in the corridor could hear them. "You'd think she'd *do something* about her hair and makeup," Veronica Grayson bored in. "And especially her clothes."

"What hair and makeup and clothes?" Claudia English sniped. "That stupid braid of hers makes her look like a farmhand, and she wouldn't know how to use makeup if you handed it to her." The girls nodded to each other, snickering nastily.

But Claudia wasn't finished. "And where does she get those clothes? They're horrid! Straight from Sears Roebuck— or worse. She has no style, no taste."

"And she doesn't even have a mother," a wannabe on the outskirts of the group chimed in—a comment so crass and uncalled for that it was all I could do to keep from screaming.

"Ignore them. Just ignore them," I repeated to myself. "If you say or do anything, it'll just make matters worse." I couldn't walk away fast enough, but like hens pecking at an outcast of their flock, the girls pursued me, ready to go in for the kill.

"No wonder she doesn't have a boyfriend," Mary Ann chortled. "Who'd wanna date a hick like that?"

"Hick? Hick?" Why, those girls didn't know one blessed thing about me—what I did, what I thought about, or what I dreamed of doing! Not that any of that would have mattered.

Mercifully, the bell rang, and everybody dispersed to go to their classes. Shaken, I continued down the hallway. I'd had high hopes for this school year. No longer a lowly freshman, I'd looked forward to getting a new start on life at Plainfield High. But now, a month into the academic year, things seemed to be the same—or even worse.

To add to my misery, my classes were of minimal interest. My geometry and natural science courses were all right, and physical education was sometimes fun. But Mr. Boyd's discussions of nineteenth-century industrialization in U.S. History were so mind-numbing I could barely keep my eyes open. And in Mrs. Jenkins's Advanced English Literature course, we'd just begun a unit on Milton's *Paradise Lost* that seemed of little relevance to my day-to-day concerns.

Even my sixth-period art class—a class where I should have excelled—was frustrating. The new teacher, Ms. MacLerren, was less than complimentary about my work. Though she praised my technical ability—acknowledging that I was more advanced than anyone else in her classes—she criticized my projects for being unimaginative and lacking passion. "You can do better," she'd told me on more than one occasion. "Much, much better."

"What more does she *want?*" I would say to myself. "I'm doing the best I can!"

I wanted to please Ms. MacLerren, not only because I wanted to improve as an artist but because I liked her and wanted her to like me, too.

Madelyn MacLerren was different from anyone I'd ever met. In her late thirties, she was tall and slim and had a distinctive flair about her. She was a woman who knew what she wanted and wasn't shy about expressing her opinions or insisting that others measure up to her expectations. She moved confidently around the room, the picture of professionalism with her long blond hair swept up into a French twist. Her clothing—nothing too ostentatious or trendy or artsy—was put together in intriguing ways. She wore well-made skirts and dresses and jackets and sweaters—predominantly in beiges and grays but also in soft purples, teals, and navies—which she paired with colorful shirts or blouses, bright scarves or belts, or unusual necklaces, pins, or earrings to contrast with her garments' muted tones.

As I walked home after school that afternoon, I was still fuming about the day's events—so much so that I thought twice about stopping for my regular weekly visit with my friends Doc and Ruby Bea Harris. But I knew they counted on my coming. As I approached their home, I made an effort to compose myself. Though Ruby Bea had heard plenty of my complaints over the years, I didn't want to burden her with the dreadful details of my latest experiences at school. She had enough problems to deal with, thanks to Doc's failing health—several minor strokes and blood clots lodged in his legs—and his flagging spirits after he'd been forced to retire from practicing medicine.

In truth, Ruby Bea's life hadn't been easy. She'd once let slip that she'd been widowed during the Depression and left to raise an infant daughter. She'd met Doc while he was caring for her mother, who was critically ill with congestive heart failure. Eventually, they'd fallen in love and married. When a call went out for doctors to come to Plainfield to provide medical care for the region, Doc was the first to arrive and set up a practice. After other doctors and nurses filtered in, they established a clinic, then a hospital. Ruby Bea had helped Doc with his practice until she was so pregnant with their fourth child that she could barely move.

It hadn't been easy then or in the intervening years. While Doc dedicated himself to medicine, Ruby Bea raised their children and tried to keep the home fires burning, no matter what the circumstances. And no telling what was in store for her now that Doc required special care.

In spite of my efforts to stifle my anger, Ruby Bea could tell I was upset. "What's the matter?" she asked.

"Nothing."

My friend pressed on. "I know well and good something's bothering you."

"I hate them!" I exploded.

"Hate who?" Ruby Bea replied. Doc, sitting in a chair nearby, stopped knocking out his pipe and looked over at me.

"I hate those girls, I hate school, and I hate myself and everything in my life!"

Doc grunted something unintelligible. Ruby Bea held her ground. "Would you care to elaborate?"

"I just get so angry," I sputtered. "I can't do *anything* right!"

"Oh?"

"My classes are so boring I can barely stay awake in them. And in my art class—which I should love—Ms. MacLerren says that I'm not living up to my potential."

Ruby Bea raised her eyebrows.

"She likes my technique but says my work is unimaginative."

"Oh dear," Ruby Bea sighed. "But I wouldn't take that too much to heart. I'll bet she sees that you've got artistic ability and wants to push you to do better."

"Maybe," I conceded. "But I don't know what she wants from me."

"Have you tried asking her?"

"Nooooo."

"Well?"

But now that the floodgates of my angst had opened, there was no stopping the rush of my resentment. "That's not the even the worst of it. The popular girls at school are always picking on me!"

"They are? Why?"

"I don't fit in."

Ruby Bea waited for me to explain.

"It's not that I want to be like them," I began. "Who would? They're snobby and mean. But I don't even like what *normal* girls are supposed to like. The things they're concerned about—boys, makeup, hairstyles, clothes—seem silly and meaningless." I glanced sideways at Ruby Bea, who continued to listen impassively. "I *do* try to look decent when I go out in public," I said, "but I *refuse* to fuss over my appearance or spend hours primping in front of the mirror the way a lot of the other girls do. And though I like boys well enough, I don't fawn over them or want to attract them, much less go out with them."

"What's wrong with not wanting to do that?"

"It makes me odd."

"At your age, that's *anything* but odd."

"Well, that's what the popular girls call me, right to my face. God knows what they say behind my back!"

"Oh?"

"They say my clothes and hair make me look like I'm from the sticks—and that I should stop spending so much time drawing and fix myself up. 'No wonder nobody wants to ask her out,' they say. As if that's the most important thing in life: having a boyfriend and going out on dates! My God! I don't think Pop would even *let* me date!" I paused to catch my breath before I went on. "I'm sure they'd be horrified if they knew that I don't have any interest in getting married or being a mother. I don't want a baby now, and I can't imagine wanting one anytime in the future."

"There's plenty of time for all that."

"But what if I *never* do?"

"Then so be it. I don't know of any law that says you have to conform to any of this. Maybe you'll choose to live your life differently."

"What do you mean?"

"Well, for example, if you develop your talent as an artist, you may end up focusing on a career."

"But—"

Ruby Bea took my hands into hers. "Hallie, you need to think about what *you* want in your life, regardless of what anybody thinks you *should* want—or be."

"But—"

"But nothing," she shot back. "The greatest freedom in the world—the greatest security and peace of mind and happiness—comes from knowing who you are and being true to yourself. Then nasty comments from people like those stuck-up girls can't touch you." She squeezed my hands to accentuate her point before going on. "But first, you have to figure out who you are and what you want—and then live your life accordingly." She stopped and looked at me pointedly. "There's nothing in the world to prevent you from choosing the way you want to live."

"And just how am I supposed to do that?" I grumbled.

Ruby Bea chuckled at my grumpiness, then said, "Even though your father controls most of your life right now, you already have more freedom in some of the choices you make than you might imagine. You'll have even more as an adult."

"Oh, really?" I said skeptically.

"You need to think about what you can do right now that'll help you become the woman you want to be and have the life you want to have. At the risk of sounding like a broken record, let me repeat that the greatest freedom in life comes from knowing who you really are and what you want to do and making choices that will get you there. Trust me, as you get older and more experienced, you'll come to understand that and make the decisions that'll let you get what you want out of life. Until then, maybe I can help."

She was as good as her word, as I would soon find out.

"Follow me," Ruby Bea said a week later when I arrived for my next visit. She guided me into a guest bedroom. I'd never seen a room so beautiful and serene. It was uncluttered and lovely, with pale yellow walls and matching drapes. A peach-colored bedspread covered the double bed, and there was an area rug in shades of peach, cream, and beige on the wood floor.

A large black trunk was sitting on the rug. Ruby Bea undid its clasps and opened it. Then, one by one, she brought out jumpers, skirts, sweaters, and blouses and laid them out on the bed. "Our daughter Marci outgrew these things some time ago," she told me. "Maybe you can use some of them."

Every item was in perfect condition and of higher quality than anything I'd ever owned or could imagine purchasing in Plainfield. Shopping in Springfield, the nearest major city, had always been out of the question because it was a good hundred miles away and most of Pop's income went toward building up our farm.

Since Mama's death, I'd made do with hand-me-down overalls and raggedy T-shirts for work around the farm. All my other clothes I purchased from Robertson's Dry Goods in town or ordered from the Sears Roebuck catalog. They were decent and serviceable, but hardly stylish. That didn't bother me most of the time, but every now and then I yearned to own something fashionable and nice.

It wasn't that I craved beauty or longed to be trendy like other girls. But every so often I would feel uneasy inside, painfully aware of all the things I didn't have. In Ruby Bea's guest bedroom that afternoon, looking over the exquisite garments laid out before me, those feelings came over me stronger than ever.

The clothes were a treasure trove of classic women's fashions. There were wool jumpers in shades of warm brown, subdued navy, and forest green, each with a matching cardigan. There were two sweater sets with matching A-line skirts—one in a warm pumpkin color and the other a deep turquoise, the color of the Caribbean Sea that I'd seen in magazines. There were pleated skirts in what Ruby Bea referred to as Black Watch and Stewart plaids and another the color of autumn leaves. Each skirt had a v-neck pullover to go with it.

Underneath the woolens were blouses—both long- and short-sleeved—in shades of cream, ochre, and white. There were also several cotton print skirts—perfect for spring and summer weather—and two cotton dresses: an A-line of turquoise floral and a more full-skirted number in shades of peach.

I was blown away—I was being given an entire new wardrobe!

They were from Marci Harris's high school years. Ruby Bea said she'd recently come across the storage trunk and thought the clothes might fit me. "I don't know why I held onto them," she said. "Maybe I thought one of the grandchildren might use them—but they all turned out to be boys. Could be I just didn't want to let go of them because Marci was our youngest."

"You don't think she'll mind?" I asked, overwhelmed by the generous gift.

"Mind?" Ruby Bea hooted. "She'll be thrilled to death to know someone can use them. What happened was that Marci had what my friend Lil—you know Lillian Pinkerton from church—and I refer to as a 'sudden growth spurt.' In other words she 'filled out fast' shortly after we bought most of this stuff. She got taller and heavier and curvier. For a while, she thought she might trim down and get back into them. But she never did. And now she's a grown woman."

"Maybe I'll be too big, too," I said.

"I doubt it." Ruby Bea looked me affectionately. "You're wiry! Well-built but slender!"

I didn't know what to say.

"Now," Ruby Bea continued, holding up the brown wool jumper, "Let's see how this looks on you." She left the room, saying "Come out and show us when you're ready."

I looked through the layers of clothing laid out on the bed and chose a long-sleeved blouse to put on underneath the jumper. With something close to reverence, I slipped my arms into the soft, smooth cotton, savoring the feel of the fabric against my skin and admiring the delicate creamy-white color of it: the color and texture of the buttercups Mama used to hold up under my chin when I was a little girl. "Make a wish!" she'd say. "Make a wish!"

The blouse felt as if it was caressing my arms and torso. I paused to luxuriate in the feeling. Then I reached for the jumper and pulled it on over my head. I held my breath as I adjusted it to fit the curves of my body. The texture was soft and smooth, and it seemed to fit perfectly. I pirouetted in front of a mirror, trying to come to terms with the vision I saw reflected. Was this really me? I looked so polished, so poised!

And more. A sense of calmness came over me, as if my inner and outer lives were suddenly more integrated, more in balance. I almost teared up.

"How're you doing in there?" Ruby Bea interrupted my reverie.

"Fine," I said as I opened the door and stepped out. I felt like a different person—a more grown-up and well-put-together person.

"Let's have a look at you," Ruby Bea said. As I walked across the room I could see a grin of approval around the pipe Doc Harris held clenched between his teeth. I nodded to him as I passed his chair and kept walking toward Ruby Bea. Then I stopped and turned in front of the older woman, who smoothed the body of the jumper with practiced hands. "Why, this outfit looks like it was made for you," she said. "It's a bit too long, but other than that it fits you perfectly!"

She sat back and took a long look at me before saying, "Now, let's see the rest."

As if in a dream, I tried on sweaters and blouses and skirts, one after another—each one neatly fitting my figure.

"Everything looks great on you," Ruby Bea said. "But I think we'd better shorten the skirts to make them more up-to-date. Hemlines these days are a lot shorter than they were a decade ago. Before you leave, I'll mark some of the skirts, so I can take them up this week."

"You're not going to turn them into mini-skirts, are you?" Doc protested, puffing vigorously on his pipe. "They don't leave much to the imagination!"

"No," Ruby Bea chuckled. "Not that short. But to look in fashion, they ought to hit two or maybe three inches above the knees." She went on. "I also think we need to pick up a few turtlenecks to update your look when you wear the jumpers and sweaters. In a couple of weeks, Doc has a doctor's appointment in Springfield. You can come along and pick them out. In the meantime, why don't you look in the five-and-dime for some cute earrings—and maybe a belt or two. You could also check to see what kind of accessories they have at Robertson's. And find out what Sherman's Drugs has in the way of makeup."

"Makeup! Pop would never let me. . . ."

"I'm not talking about heavy makeup," Ruby Bea cut in. "But a bit of lightly tinted lip gloss might be nice—Yardley Pot o' Gloss seems to be the rage right now—and maybe a little eyeliner or eye shadow or mascara to try out. Bonne Bell makes cosmetics with teenagers like you in mind."

As I was pulled deeper into the plans for my makeover, I began to feel excited about my prospects—until I looked at my feet. My penny loafers seemed hopelessly out of place amidst all the finery. Noticing my discomfort, Ruby Bea spoke up. "Shoes—maybe even boots—we can deal with later. Your loafers are fine for the time being, particularly if you keep them polished and get some tights to wear with them." She paused to consider. "You know, most of the clothes you have right now aren't bad. They just need some updating with shorter hems, newer shirts or blouses, and some accessories to give them a little pizzazz." She winked at me. "When we get through with you, those snippy girls won't know what hit 'em!"

All too soon, it was time for me to head home and make supper. It was then I felt my first moments of panic. How would Pop react to the clothes and all the plans?

Ruby Bea had already anticipated that this might be a problem. "I'll talk with your father about all this," she said, "so he isn't worried or offended."

I smiled. I knew for a fact that Ruby Bea would make Pop understand. In her own quiet way, she was a force to be reckoned with. "Steel fist in a velvet glove" was how I'd once heard her best friend Lil describe her, adding that "if Ruby Bea wants to get something done, it sure as hell *gets* done. And people are more than happy to do it."

That turned out to be the case with Pop. He grumbled at first, but after some back-and-forth he accepted Ruby Bea's remarkable gift and gave me the money I needed for accessories. "Just don't get anything crazy," he warned.

Right away, my new look got noticed in school.

"Will you look at that?" Priscilla Harper shrilled as soon as she spotted me.

"Gawd-A'mighty! What happened to *her*?" somebody else chimed in. I knew the eyes of every popular girl were focused on me as I swept past them, making my way to my locker.

Already I felt more confident, as if my new clothes had provided me with armor against the slings and arrows—and mean comments—of the world. All of a sudden, my old self seemed to be disappearing. "Good riddance," I thought. That old self had left me pretty much defenseless against the popular girls and all the other bad things in my life. "That," I resolved, "was never going to be the case again."

Over the following weeks, I found myself going to my closet every afternoon after school, taking out my new outfits and spreading them out on my bed. As I sat stroking the fabrics and admiring them, I began to notice that their various colors were having different effects on me.

I noticed that light blues tended to make me feel sort of dreamy and expansive—darker shades of blue, quiet and reflective. Golds and russets gave me a warm, energized feeling. The browns generated a sense of security, calmness, and solidity. Greens brought out a range of responses. Forest or spruce evoked mystery and depth; pastel greens felt lighter and airier; limes and chartreuses created alarm. True reds made me feel alert and assertive; orangey reds, messy and hot. Pinks radiated quietness and sensitivity, while the darker rose hues made me feel calm and quiet and tender and vulnerable. Grays seemed subdued and pensive; blacks produced a serious, self-assured mood, a sense of controlled power that seemed to say "Don't mess with me!"

And it suddenly occurred to me: if colors could influence my moods and attitudes, they could have the same effect on my artwork. By using color in a well-thought-out way, I could enhance a work's impact on the viewer by helping emphasize the appropriate "mood" that I was trying to express: warm and pleasant, deep and mysterious, menacing and scary, whatever.

At the same time, as I looked over my new wardrobe, I began to feel a new awareness of line and contour, and how different textures and fabrics produced different shadings of color tone. All of a sudden, my new clothes were not only boosting my self-confidence—they were giving me a more complex new artistic aesthetic.

My new attire and attitude quickly got noticed not only by the popular girls but by Ms. MacLerren. Along with updating my clothing, I had begun to apply some of my new awareness to my art projects for school. Instead of drawing exact likenesses in conventional colors, I began experimenting with form and color tone: a single Day-Glo yellow flower floating in a soft olive sky, a psychedelic butterfly in a snowy-white field.

"You look very nice," Ms. MacLerren remarked to me one day as she was making the rounds of the classroom. "And I like what you're beginning to do with your work." Later, as

I was leaving the classroom, she stopped me. "Keep going farther, Hallie. Let yourself go!"

Several weeks later, Ms. MacLerren stopped me again. "I liked that blood-red spider you did in pen and ink and watercolor," she said. "I've never seen anything quite like it. It not only draws the viewer in with its visual impact, it also has a visceral quality to it. And placing the spider in the palm of that gnarly gray hand works very effectively. It evokes some unspoken backstory—especially with the long, veined arm extending off the page. In fact, it's interesting and original enough that I think you ought to enter it in the regional student art competition up in Springfield next month. I'm one of the judges, so you can ride up with me."

In her car on the way to the event, she asked me about the recent transformation of my appearance and my approach to my artwork.

"Something seemed to happen to me when my friend Ruby Bea Harris gave me a bunch of clothes," I began.

"They certainly made a dramatic difference in your appearance."

"Not just my appearance," I said. "After I put them on, I began to feel more grown-up, more self-confident."

"Amazing, isn't it, how something as simple as finding the right clothes can make *such* a difference?"

"I never realized it before," I said. "You know, I've always admired the way you dress. You always look so well-put-together and at ease with yourself."

"Thanks," she responded, "but you wouldn't *believe* how long it took me to assemble a wardrobe that created the impression I wanted to make, the image I wanted to convey. It took more thought and attention than you can imagine and a lot of trial and error." She paused and smiled at me. "But I want to hear more about what happened to you."

"Well, there was something about the colors and cuts and textures of those clothes that spoke to me in ways I can't even describe. They made me see things differently. And I guess some of that's starting to come out in the stuff I'm drawing and painting. Crazy, huh?"

"It's not crazy at all. In fact, it's important."

"What do you mean?"

"You're starting to see the world through an artist's eyes, Hallie. Keep it up and you could end up becoming a professional artist one day."

She looked at me and smiled. "What you need is more practice and more training and more experience working with the materials and techniques that'll help you acquire the skill and sophistication—and the self-confidence—you need."

"I've got so much to learn," I groaned.

"You'll learn it," Ms. MacLerren replied. "Trust your instincts and your intuition. I can tell you're already starting to do that. Pretty soon you'll have a better sense of who you are and what you can do."

"Ruby Bea said something like that to me."

"What did she say?"

"I was telling her that I wasn't a normal girl and didn't fit in. I don't care about the stuff other girls my age care about."

"And she said?"

"She asked if 'fitting in' was what was most important to me."

"And . . . ?"

"She said I needed to worry less about fitting in and think more about who I was and what I really want to do with my life and how best to get it."

"She's right, you know," Ms. MacLerren said as she maneuvered her car into the parking lot of the Springfield Armory, where the student competition was about to begin.

I'd never seen an auditorium so large or so full of people, all acting as if they knew exactly what to do and where to go. "Remember: you belong here, too," Ms. MacLerren reminded me as she headed off to join the other judges.

The other students' works were really good—intimidatingly good. "I don't have a snowball's chance in Hell," I said to myself as I made my way around the auditorium, studying each entry. A wide range of different media and different styles of art was represented. And yet my spider composition didn't look entirely out of place among them.

As I surveyed the room, I also noticed that many of the other student artists appeared to be just as nervous as I was. It was obvious, too, that they were just as serious about their work and were genuinely interested in seeing what the other contestants had created.

"Kindred souls," I thought. "No matter what happens here, maybe this is the world I belong in."

The judges took their time looking over our work, examining our entries all morning before taking a break for lunch. Then they went back at it until late afternoon. The tension in the auditorium kept building until, finally, there was the awards ceremony. To my disbelief, I was first runner-up in the mixed-media category. My knees shook as I accepted my award. I could see Ms. MacLerren beaming.

While we were walking back to her car, she hugged me and said she was proud of me. She said there'd been discussion among the judges about whether I should get first prize or whether the top honor should go to a senior boy from a private school in Springfield. In the end, they decided his entry was slightly more accomplished and sophisticated—although as far as she was concerned it was much less imaginative.

"Looks like you're on your way, Hallie Jo Everheart!" she said. "From now on, I'm going to push you even harder, whether you like it or not!"

On the drive back to Plainfield, we resumed our earlier conversation. "You know, your friend Ruby Bea is right!" Ms. MacLerren remarked.

"How do you mean?"

"About fitting in. You need to realize that there's more than one way to be a girl or a woman. I think that's what your friend was trying to tell you. The fact is, you may very well end up deciding to be an artist instead of a wife and mother—and it's perfectly all right, and perfectly *normal*, if you do. You might choose never to marry, or you might end up in some sort of unconventional arrangement. Lots of women in the arts have." She explained that Georgia O'Keeffe had never had children. And although she married Alfred Stieglitz, the celebrated New York City photographer, she lived apart from him many months of the year because she wanted to work where she found the most inspiration. "And unless I'm mistaken, she's still living and working out in the mountains of New Mexico.

"And speaking of O'Keeffe, did you know that she's also very particular about her clothing? She designs many of her own outfits so she can have precisely the look she wants. At some point early on, she decided to dress almost entirely in black and white—black for the colder months and white for the warmer ones. In fact, her clothes became one of her trademarks, part of her carefully cultivated public persona. And there have been plenty of other female artists who've found fulfillment in their lives, and freedom from society's expectations, by devoting themselves to their work instead of marrying and having families."

"Did you choose to devote yourself to your art and not marry?" I asked.

Ms. MacLerren grew quiet. "Actually, I was married once." She looked as if she'd disclosed more than she wanted to, as if I'd opened a topic that might be too private and too painful to talk about.

I kept quiet until she finally spoke again. "I really don't like to talk about this, and I almost never do," she began tentatively, "but I suppose I'd better explain. I trust that you'll keep what I'm about to say strictly between us."

While living in New York City, Ms. MacLerren had met and married a man named Scott Barron when they were completing MFAs at Columbia. Both of them were determined to become professional artists. But it proved to be almost impossible to support themselves solely from selling their artwork. Over time, her husband began drinking heavily and became abusive—enraged that the world didn't recognize his genius or reward him for his talent. At first, the abuse was verbal; but it eventually turned physical. One night, he knocked her down and grabbed her by the throat. By the grace of God, she got away and left him and went to live with her sister in Springfield, Missouri. She'd hoped to find a position at the state university there. But when nothing became available, she jumped at the opportunity to teach art at Plainfield High School. And now here she was—taking me under her wing.

I was quiet after my teacher finished her story, lost in my own thoughts. My mind was suddenly reeling with new possibilities. As I looked down at the award certificate in my lap, I began to get a new sense of who I was and what I wanted to do in life. I suddenly knew that I wanted to be a professional artist, and that I might actually have the potential to become one.

And then it was Monday, and I was back at school.

The popular girls were in the hallway, as usual, looking for victims to abuse with their cattiness. As I exited the girl's bathroom, Claudia English said, "Well, she looks better, but she's still really odd." A murmur of agreement followed.

I stopped, turned, and stared at the group with an amused look on my face—as if their opinions were much too silly and insignificant for words. "Morons!" I said and walked away smiling.

Losing Matthew

*A*T THE END OF MY SOPHOMORE YEAR in high school, I unexpectedly acquired a stepmother and a new bedroom. Following a whirlwind five-month romance in 1967, my father had married Doris Weston, a member of his church congregation and the sister of Roxanne Jones, the owner of the local diner. Doris was a widow with four sons, three of whom—nine-year-old twins and an eleven-year-old—were still living with her. Which meant that space in our farmhouse was going to be tight. To deal with an overcrowded and potentially awkward situation, Pop decided to build a one-room extension off the west side of the farmhouse and let me move into it.

The new room was completed a couple of weeks before Pop and Doris's May wedding. "Come see what we've fixed up for you!" Pop said, guiding me through the kitchen, past his office and the downstairs bathroom to the end of a newly extended hallway; Spirit, my golden retriever, followed at our heels, her tail wagging and her toenails clicking a rhythmic beat on the bare wood floor.

Pop opened a door and stepped into the spacious new room, pulling me in behind him. "What do you think? I know it's not completely finished—it still needs paint and moldings around the doors and windows—but it's finished enough for you to move into."

The room was almost twice the size of my old bedroom and smelled fresh and sweet with the scents of new pine and drywall. Spirit sneezed heartily, signifying her satisfaction. "Well, I guess we know what *she* thinks!" Pop remarked. "I'll move her bedding down here as soon as you like."

A bed had been set up in a far corner of the room—a four-poster that Pop had found in the attic and resurrected with a thorough cleaning and a new mattress. The frame was well over a century old and made of solid oak stained dark. It fastened together with wooden pegs and sat high off the floor. On the opposite side of the room was a large library table, well-worn but functional. Above it were shelves to store my art supplies and books.

I walked over to two of the room's windows and stroked the smooth white curtains—as soft as my white cotton nightgown.

"Doris made those for you," Pop said. "She brought them by this afternoon. She said she chose white because it would go with whatever color you paint the walls. They can also be dyed any color you want."

"They're lovely," I said, finding my voice. "The whole room is lovely!" I raised one of the windows, and late April rushed in, bringing birdsong and the fragrance of crocus, jonquils, and newly emerging leaves and grasses. Spirit's head went up. Her nose quivered as she sniffed the multitude of intriguing scents. From this window, I could see the yard and garden and fields all the way to where they dipped downward toward our pond. Beyond that were our woods and, in the distance, the foothills of the Ozark Mountains.

I turned and surveyed the room. To my left was another pair of windows and next to them a door to the outside, the upper portion of which was set with small, diamond-shaped panes of glass. "What's this?"

"I had a private entrance made for you. You get moody, sometimes, just like me."

I grimaced.

"You know you do! I've seen you outside, pacing back and forth in a snit about something or other. This way, you can go in and out whenever you like."

I couldn't believe my ears. Was Pop—the man who, for the past seven years had monitored practically every move of my life—now telling me that he'd actually planned a way for me to leave unnoticed?

I opened the door and looked out onto a small porch with a span of yellow pine steps leading down to the lawn. Like the room, they smelled of new wood and springtime. I felt a flood of affection for my father. "It's *beautiful*, Pop! It's all wonderful!"

"Sure you won't get lonely?" my father teased.

Lonely? Why on earth would I feel lonely? I was about to complete my second year at Plainfield High School. Spirit—a stray I'd nursed back to health—had become my constant companion. And Pop was finally getting remarried, to a joyous and loving woman who was strong and energetic and pretty. Pop seemed happier than I'd seen him in years. In the five months since he'd gotten serious about Doris, the deepest lines in his face had smoothed, and he walked taller and straighter and stronger. And he seemed undaunted by the challenge of raising her three young boys.

Still, I couldn't help but have mixed feelings about vacating my old room—the room Mama had fixed up for me a year and a half before she died. That bedroom and everything in it were tangible reminders of how much she'd loved and cared for me.

"Everything will be fine," I told myself. But because my new room was a splendid one that Pop had planned with all my needs in mind as a present for my sixteenth birthday, I wanted to sound appreciative. And I *was* appreciative. It was just that all these changes would take some getting used to.

Changes? There'd been plenty of them, with more coming all the time. Our small Ozark community, like the rest of small-town rural Middle America in 1967, wasn't immune to all that was happening in the world. The war in Vietnam was escalating. Young men were being called up to serve in the military. One of my brothers, Drew, had enlisted, and the other, Eddie, was somewhere in Canada. Antiwar protests were exploding on college campuses, and hippie flower-children were experimenting with free love in San Francisco. And just a few years earlier, a presidential assassination had traumatized the nation.

World-shaking events, played out before our eyes on the TV news broadcasts of Huntley-Brinkley and Walter Cronkite, were happening so fast that it seemed as if life as we'd known it was breaking apart and, like Humpty Dumpty, would never be put back together again.

But now here was Pop, standing next to me in my new room and trying his best to make my life a happy—or at least a normal—one. "No, Pop. I won't be lonely," I said, embracing him. "And thanks, Pop. Thanks for everything. Tell Doris thanks, too. It's *perfect* in every way."

Matthew entered my life and my room that summer, slipping in through my private entrance. He was Doris's oldest son and had just turned nineteen. He'd been living in St. Louis with an uncle—initially to finish high school, then to work at odd jobs while attending classes at a local community college—when he decided to come south to Plainfield and work on our farm while he figured out what to do with his life.

In early spring, the challenge was always the same for small farmers like Pop: find a crew of good men to help with the plowing and planting. The previous year, he'd contracted with our local county group home to hire young men who'd had run-ins with the law. They were brought in every day to work as part of a rehabilitation program as an alternative to jail, and most of them proved to be conscientious laborers. As a result, when Matthew suddenly showed up on the doorstep in early June, Pop already had a work crew in place. Pop nevertheless offered Matthew a job and a small apartment—really a storeroom converted into an office-apartment—upstairs in our newly renovated barn.

The first time I met my new stepbrother was at Pop and Doris's wedding. Though we didn't have much opportunity to talk before or after the ceremony, I studied him off and on for most of the day. He was tall and muscular, and he moved among the guests with athletic grace. A lock of dark brown hair continually fell across his eyes. He seemed soft-spoken and polite, with a smile that was tentative at first but widened to illuminate his entire face when he was happy.

He also had the habit of looking directly at a person when he was talking to them—a trait that had so unnerved me when we were introduced that I'd been too tongue-tied to speak. Except for Pop, I thought Matthew was the handsomest man—if a nineteen-year-old could be called a man—I'd ever seen.

When he moved in with us, all he brought with him was an oversized khaki duffle bag and a guitar. He immediately went to work, pinching off strawberry runners in the fields. I didn't see him during the daytime, but he sat directly across from me at supper time.

One night, a couple of weeks after his arrival, I heard a guitar. I looked up from a sketch I'd been working on and put down my pencil. I listened closely, trying to pick out a melody, but all I could hear was muted sound drifting through my open bedroom window. I pushed back from my worktable and went to the window to try to locate the source of the music. Spirit, asleep on her bed in the corner, raised her head and yawned, then laid her head back down. Pulling back the curtain, I looked out.

At first, all I could see was a flurry of fireflies, flickering on and off against the darkness of the night, and a steady glow of light coming from the barn. Then I saw Matthew.

He was sitting on the top rung of an old wooden fence near the barn, curled around the body of his guitar, fingering the strings like a modern-day troubadour in work boots and blue jeans. I stood watching him at the window until, overcome by the romance of it all, I dropped the curtain and flipped off the light. I slid out of my jeans and T-shirt and into my nightgown, and after climbing into bed, I lay listening to the faint, other-worldly sound of his guitar until I fell asleep.

Several nights later, I saw Matthew walking in the moonlight. As before, I switched off the light and got into bed. Stretching out on top of the covers, I pulled back the curtain and looked out into the night.

The white oaks and elms that dotted our yard were silhouetted against the sky. It was a clear night and the stars were so bright a person could easily pick out the constellations. The moon, almost full, filled a top corner of my window.

I was startled to see Matthew step out from under one of the elms. He glided through the yard like a phantom, walked to the fence bordering the yard, then stopped, leaned against it, and looked out across the fields. I watched him, fascinated, but also feeling like a voyeur, intruding into an intimate part of his life. When he turned and looked at the house, I froze, wondering if he could see me or hear the loud thump of my heart beating so hard and fast that I thought I might faint. I held my breath until he turned toward the fields.

I closed the curtain and crawled between my sheets, lying awake in the darkness until I finally managed to fall asleep.

Then it was morning with a summery breeze blowing through the open window, lifting the curtain and letting sunlight dance on the walls of my still unfinished room.

That day, I thought about Matthew as I went about my chores. Spirit seemed to sense that I was distracted and would barely leave my side.

At supper that night, I was too embarrassed to make eye-contact with my stepbrother. As soon as I helped wash the dishes, I retreated to my room. But when I tried to begin a new drawing, all I could do was scribble aimlessly on the page. In frustration, I put down my pencil and picked up a book. Try as I might, however, I just couldn't concentrate.

I debated whether or not to pull back the curtain. "What if he's out there? What'll I do then?" I asked Spirit, who had jumped up beside me on the bed. Finally, I turned off the lamp, pulled back the curtain, and looked out into the yard. There was Matthew, leaning against the elm nearest my window. "Hi," he said.

Spirit roused herself and growled softly. "It's okay, girl," I said.

Matthew straightened up and walked over to me. From where he stood, his head was even with the window sill. He stood there for a moment, looking down at the ground and not saying a word, kicking at a tuft of grass with the toe of his boot. Finally, he looked up and said, "Didn't I see you looking out your window last night? I thought I saw you when I was out walking."

I ran my hand nervously along the windowsill and decided to tell the truth.

"You did. But I wasn't spying on you; I just like looking out at the moon."

"Me too," he said. "It's why I came out last night. Tonight, too, though I was sort of hoping you'd look out again. We haven't had much of a chance to talk."

"I guess I spend a lot of time in my room."

"What do you do in there?"

"I read, study, the usual. Mostly, I draw."

"So you're an artist?"

"Well, I can't really call myself one yet. But I want to be. I've been drawing for almost as long as I can remember."

"Can I see some of them?"

"I guess so, if you really want to."

He reached out to stop the nervous fidgeting of my hand. "When?"

I hesitated, then heard myself say, "Well, I suppose you could come in and see them now. Go 'round to the side of the house; I've got a private entrance."

When I heard Matthew's footsteps on the porch outside the door, I was so nervous I thought my heart might jump out of my chest. I took a few deep breaths to compose myself while Spirit trotted to the door, woofing softly.

Matthew stepped into the room. Spirit sniffed his boots thoroughly. "Good dog," he said, bending down to pet her and scratch her ears. "Good girl."

Then he straightened up, and began walking around the room, surveying its contents. He stopped at my work table. "Pop got that for me a few months ago," I said. "He found it at an auction."

Matthew continued to explore the room, stopping to admire the curtains.

"Your Mom made those," I told him.

He turned to me and smiled. "It all looks great!"

"Well, it's not finished yet. The doors and windows still need trim, and the whole room needs to be painted."

"Maybe I can help. Do you know what color you want?"

"Ivory," I said. "It has to be ivory."

"Then ivory it'll be." He returned to the worktable and bent over it, fingering some of my pencil sketches spread out there. "You did these?" I nodded. He picked up one of them and studied it closely.

"That's a sketch of the pond down beyond the pasture; I'm not quite finished with it," I said, taking it from him. "Let me show you some of the others." I took a portfolio from one of the shelves, pulled out some pastoral scenes I'd done in ink and watercolors, and spread them on the table.

He looked carefully at each one. "These are unusual— they're really *good*. Do you have any more?"

I reached up to the top shelf and took down another portfolio. "These are some other things I'm working on. Nobody's ever seen them." I reached into the portfolio and eased out a series of drawings done in charcoal. They were face portraits of an attractive woman who bore a resemblance to me.

"These are *amazing!*"

"They're my mother," I said. "I started them about a year ago. They're not very good yet—just preliminary sketches—but I'll keep working on them. I don't want anyone to even know about them until they're right."

"But they look perfect right now!"

"They still need a *lot* of work. I haven't been able to capture her spirit yet!" I gathered the portraits, slipped them into the portfolio, and placed it back on the top shelf. Matthew slid the watercolors into their portfolio, then turned to face me. "I'd better go."

"Do you have to?"

"Yeah. It's getting late. And tomorrow's a work day."

I fiddled with the folds of my robe, mumbling, "Maybe you can come back sometime."

"Sure, if you want me to."

"Tomorrow?"

He nodded, then slipped out the door.

Over the next two months, we met almost every night—whenever Matthew could get away without attracting attention. Painting my room provided us with an excuse to be together. After supper, the two of us would adjourn to my room. There, working side by side with paint bushes in hand, we'd talk. I'd always been shy and introverted, but I now found myself opening up. It was as if I'd been starved to talk with somebody my own age—a boy, no less!—and share my thoughts and plans and dreams.

After the room was painted, our conversations continued—uninhibited, dreamy conversations that followed whatever random thoughts popped into our heads.

"You don't get away from this farm very much, do you?" he asked me one night. We were sitting in the muted light of the lamp: he was in the straight-backed wooden chair next to my worktable, and I was in the nearby rocker. Spirit snored softly in her bed, nearby. The room still smelled lightly of paint.

"No," I said. "When Mama was alive, we went once or twice to visit Pop's mother in Kansas City. And every chance we'd get, we'd come down here from Springfield to visit her Uncle Grant, who owned this place before he died and Mama inherited it. After Mama died, Pop was still trying to get the farm established, so we had to stay here to work."

"How'd your mother die, anyway?"

"Cancer. She had it a little more than a year."

"I figured something like that. Must've been hard."

"It changed a lot of things," I responded. "Pop never said much. But I could tell he was devastated, because he became very quiet and stern and terribly protective of me—I guess because I was the youngest and the only girl. He still gets worried if I stay too late after school or go off someplace without telling him. But every so often, I think about getting away. I know there's so much to see."

"Maybe you could come to St. Louis sometime—if I'm still there, that is. Right now, I'm not sure where I'll end up."

"What do you mean?"

"I'm thinking of enlisting."

"Enlisting!"

"Well, the way things are going, I'll probably be drafted before long. So I might as well sign up before I get called."

"But you might get *killed!*"

"Yeah," Matthew responded in a monotone. "But a man's supposed to do his duty. And besides, I haven't got anything better to do."

"But you could stay here or get another job until you're called up! You shouldn't have trouble finding something. And you could stay right here with us."

"I don't know. Maybe I will. But we're in a war—whether we like it or not—and I want to do my part for our country."

"Men!" I thought but didn't say a word.

The weeks went by quickly—weeks of rendezvous and conversations that meant the world to me.

"Do you believe in God?" Matthew asked me one night. We'd been lying on the bed with the window curtains tied back, looking out at the moon and stars.

I turned to face him. "Of course. Don't you?"

He stared out the window. "I dunno. There's got to be *something* out there that keeps things in order. But, what? I wish I knew for sure."

"I like to believe in God," I said. "A person's got to believe in *something*. And I like to think there's a Heaven, too, so I can see Mama again someday."

The room grew silent as we pondered the cosmic questions. Then Matthew shifted positions and looked at me. "Do you pray?"

This was a private matter: to-the-depths-of-my-soul private. "Of course," I replied. "I did a lot when Mama was sick. I thought if I prayed hard enough, maybe it would make her get better."

Matthew put his hand on my back and rubbed slowly up and down the length of it. "You were pretty young when she died, weren't you?"

"Nine," I said quietly. My thoughts turned inward. When I spoke again, my voice sounded as if it was coming from far away. "When Mama was in the hospital, we'd stay with my

Uncle Bob and Aunt Liz in Springfield. Once we stayed for nearly four weeks. Funny how what I remember most from that time is seeing groups of Catholic girls in their uniforms walking to and from school. I'd envy them because they seemed so self-assured—as if they had hold of some secret power that made them feel confident and safe. I'd see the little gold crosses they wore around their necks and think maybe *that's* what protected them: like those crosses were some sort of magic charms to ward off everything scary and mean and evil." I picked at a fingernail. "For years, I wanted something like that—something I could look at and hold whenever I felt confused or frightened."

That summer, I barely noticed when July changed to August, the hottest month of the year. I lived for the hours when Matthew came to see me. Because of the heat, the crews had to start work at dawn each morning. But after supper Matthew would come to my room, same as usual.

"It's hot, it's too hot!" I complained one evening. I was lounging on the four-poster, propped up on my elbows and talking with Matthew stretched out beside me on the bed. I sat up and gathered my hair into my hands and twisted it into a bun at the nape of my neck. "I should cut off this mop."

"Don't!" The vehemence of his reply startled me.

I released my hands and shook my head until my hair fell freely around my shoulders. "It drives me crazy in the summer."

"Lots of girls would give their eye teeth to have your hair."

"But it's so long and hot and out of control—especially when I don't wear it in a braid!" I slid off the bed and glided to the dresser across the room. I returned with a brush in my hand, which I began pulling vigorously through my thick length of honey-gold curls. "Ow-ow-ow-ow-ow!" I yelped with every stroke. Spirit rose from her bed, alarmed.

"Let me do it," Matthew said, pushing himself off the bed. I handed him the brush and lowered myself into the chair in front of my worktable. By this time, Spirit had positioned herself next to me, in order to monitor Matthew's every move. "Let me know if it pulls," he said as he began to run the brush lightly through my hair. As he continued to brush, I felt myself being lulled by the steady rhythm he fell into, brushing with one hand and smoothing with the other.

"Ummmmm!" I sighed. "I can feel the bristles clear to my scalp!"

"I'm not hurting you, am I?"

"No, it feels kind of like a massage."

Matthew continued to brush—slowly and deeply and thoroughly, long past the time it would have taken to brush out a few tangles. When he finally laid the brush on the table, I turned to him and put my arms around his waist, then leaned against him, rocking slowly back and forth while he smoothed my hair.

After that, the hair-brushing became an evening ritual. While he brushed, Matthew would sometimes stop to lift my hair and bury his face in a cloud of curls.

"'Amber waves of grain' was how Mama used to describe our hair," I told him one night. "The color of our hair was a lot alike, though hers was straighter and lighter than mine."

"'Amber waves of grain'—that's a good description," Matthew said, nodding. "It's beautiful . . . and so are you."

A few nights later, I asked, half to myself and half to Matthew, "Have you ever been in love?"

He paused to consider the matter. "Real love? I don't really know. Have you?"

"I'm not sure. I love Pop. And I loved Mama when she was still alive." I took a deep breath. "And I love you." I didn't look at him. Instead, I stared at his hands: strong, beautiful hands with long, slender fingers and rounded nails which, in spite of his work on the farm, he always kept clean. Every time I saw those hands, they stirred something inside me, making me feel oddly warm and vulnerable.

He got up from his chair, walked over to the bed, and sat down beside me. "I know you do," he said putting his arm around me, "and I think I love you, too." His voice sounded as if he was trying to control something inside. He kissed me lightly on the forehead. I smiled and put my head on his shoulder. I felt the rise and fall of his breathing, caught the rhythm, and breathed with him.

I didn't say a word, wrapped in the intimacy of the silence and wanting Matthew to be the first to speak. He sighed. "It would be so easy. . . " he began, then stopped, as if he wasn't sure what to say next or how to say it. "You know, Hallie," he resumed, "we've got to be careful." I sat up and stared at him. "I mean, you're young and pretty. We're attracted to each other, and here we are in your room. Under other circumstances we might—I mean, if you weren't my stepsister. But we can't! We just can't!"

"Have you ever made love?" I asked, my voice tentative and unsteady. "I haven't. In fact, I've never even kissed a boy. I don't understand the feelings I have when I'm with you. All I know is that I want to be close."

Matthew sucked in his breath, then let it out slowly. "That's what I'm talking about. We've got to be careful. I'm feeling the same way. But I'm . . . I'm . . . your stepbrother. We just can't!"

"But what are we going to *do*? I want to be with you. And I love it when you brush my hair and hug me."

"I know, I know. I like it, too." He paused for a minute, got up from the bed, and began pacing back and forth. "Well, I don't suppose it *all* has to stop. We just can't . . . well . . . you know . . . go all the way."

"Or get anywhere close."

"Or get anywhere close."

"We won't," I resolved. "I mean, if we make up our minds not to, we can stick to it, can't we?"

"I hope so," Matthew said solemnly.

The next two weeks we continued to meet every evening. Sometimes, if it wasn't too late, we'd sit on the porch—Spirit curled nearby—and Matthew would play his guitar. We were still drawn to each other, but we were trying hard to remain true to our vow.

Though we were careful, we weren't careful enough. One night, Pop found us together.

It was a hot, sticky, breezeless evening—the kind so typical of the Ozarks in August. The temperature had soared past one hundred degrees that day and hadn't cooled down much two hours after sunset. The cricket-sound—normally soothing—seemed deafening and grated on everyone's nerves. Restless, Pop had left Doris sleeping upstairs and had come downstairs to find a spot where it was cooler. He'd wandered outside, thinking he'd sit on the front porch.

The moon was out, a bright three-quarter moon that made the fence and trees and outbuildings look as if they were part of some surreal dream. Still restless, he'd left the porch to amble around the yard. Rounding the corner of the house, he found Matthew and me lying on a quilt we'd spread on the porch outside my room. We were both half-dozing from the heat—my hand lightly touching his shoulder and his resting on the curve of my waist. As always, Spirit was near my side. When Pop approached, she whined softly and her tail began thumping against the hard wood floor.

"What're you doing out here?" Pop's voice stabbed into the serenity of the night.

We sat up, blinking rapidly and trying to focus on the irate man standing over us. "Nothing, Pop," I said as soon as I could find my voice. "It was too hot inside, so we came out here where it's cooler."

"And what, may I ask, were you doing together *inside*?" By this time, Pop was on my porch radiating the explosiveness of an electrical storm.

"Nothing, Pop. We weren't doing anything."

Matthew got to his feet. "We were just talking, Sir. That's all. You *know* I wouldn't do anything. I'm not like that. We were looking up at the stars, and I guess we must have drifted off."

"Hmph!" Pop snorted. "I just don't know."

"Honest, Mr. Everheart," Matthew said, "we were just talking."

"Well, I'd like to believe you. Still, I think we'd better have a talk." He turned to me. "You go inside now, Hallie. Take the dog with you. And stay there." He nodded to Matthew. "Let's take a walk."

I shot a panicked look at my stepbrother. Not wanting to infuriate my father any further, I gathered the quilt and retreated to my room. I lay down on top of the bed. Spirit immediately took her place beside me. There, I watched the dark of the night turn charcoal, then gray, then silver, signaling the dawn of a new day.

I slept, but only fitfully. When I lurched awake, sunlight was streaming in through the window. Spirit was still drowsing beside me. I glanced at the clock: it was already 9 a.m.

I jumped off the bed and wriggled into some clothes. Walking toward the kitchen, I heard voices.

The next thing I saw was Matthew's duffle, lying near the back door. He was dressed in his best jeans and a sport shirt—the clothes he'd worn when he'd arrived on the farm three months before. "I've decided to go home, Hallie," Matthew said quietly. "It's time."

I turned to Pop, full of a rage I never knew I possessed. "*You* did this! *You!*" I screamed. "We weren't doing *anything* last night. Or any of the *other* nights. We were just *talking*. Is that such a *crime*?"

My tirade caught Pop off guard. "I know, I know." He stepped toward me, wanting to calm my fury.

"No, you *don't* know!" I stepped back from him. "You have *no idea* what it's like to live so far away from everybody. *You just don't know at all!*"

"It's okay, Hallie. It's okay." Matthew tried to quiet me.

I turned to Matthew. "No, it's *not* okay!" I turned back to Pop, lowering my voice, but only slightly. "Then Matthew comes along—a nice boy, somebody my age to talk to—and you have to go and *ruin* it!" I began to sob.

"Now Hallie," Pop began.

"Sssh!" Matthew soothed. By now, he was at my side. He put his hand under my chin and raised it, so I had to look at him. He appeared to be forcing himself to behave as strong and steady and manly as possible.

"Look, Hallie," he said as if measuring out his words. "It's almost the end of summer, anyway. I'd only planned to stay here until I figured out what I wanted to do."

"Well, what *do* you want to do?" I'd stopped crying, but my voice was watery.

"Like I said before, with the war on in Vietnam, it's only a matter of time until I'll be drafted. I've decided to enlist before that happens. Then, I might have some control, a little more chance for . . . what . . . I don't know. Maybe some sort of priority."

"But why now?"

"Maybe the Army's the best place for me. And if I go in now, at least I'll feel like I'm going of my own free will." When I opened my mouth to protest, his fingers tightened their grip on my shoulders and he pulled me into him, hugging me, while Pop stood by, looking vigilant and disturbed.

Finally, Pop cleared his throat. "It's time to go." He walked outside to start the pickup for the trip into town to the bus station.

Matthew hugged me one last time and kissed me right on the mouth. "I'll never forget you . . . or this summer," he whispered. Then he turned to his mother. "Better call the boys, Mom," he said, "so I can tell 'em goodbye."

Before he left, Matthew promised to write. He kept his promise, sending letters from boot camp and beyond. It couldn't have been more than a month later when a small package arrived in our mailbox, addressed to me, which I smuggled into my bedroom. Inside the package was a velvet-lined box containing a small gold cross on a chain. With it was a handwritten note: "Love, M."

Four months later, Matthew was deployed to Vietnam. After that, we received only the occasional postcard or letter. I missed him terribly, but for the most part my life went on pretty much as usual. I went to school, helped with the chores, and continued to draw.

Drawing and painting—at home and at school—helped distract me from worrying about Matthew and the ache and emptiness I felt without him. That, and the cross he'd sent me. I'd take it out every night before I went to bed and hold it tightly while I prayed with all my might, "Please, God. Please keep him safe. Please, please, *please!*" I'd kiss the cross and put it back into the box.

The telegram came one day while I was in school. I knew what had happened the minute I saw Pop standing by his pickup, waiting for me.

"Drew?" I asked.

"No, honey."

"Don't say it, Pop! For *God's sake*, don't say it!" I held up a hand, as if to shut out the news.

"I'm sorry."

We drove home in silence. When I got there, I went to my room and closed the door. In a daze, I took the velvet-lined box from the dresser, opened it, pulled out the cross, and held it in the palm of my hand. I looked at it for a very long time, then kissed it and put it back into its box. I read the note Matthew had written, repositioned it beneath the cross, and shut the container.

Then I took the box outside and down my porch steps. I walked to the large oak that stood alone at the edge of a field sprinkled with wildflowers. I knelt beneath the tree and dug a hole in the ground with my bare hands and a stick I found nearby. I placed the box in the hole and covered it. Then I stood up and wiped my hands on my skirt, not caring if I got it dirty. For several minutes, I looked at the small mound. Then I turned and walked back to my room. I went in and shut the door tight.

There, inside that ivory chamber, I started to draw and paint as if my life depended on it—which it probably did.

The days extended into weeks, then months. I took to wearing black. I chose black—rather it chose me—not because of convention but because my world had become dark, colorless, and I felt compelled to pare down to basics— absolute nothingness—so I could go inward and create a deep, dark place within me devoid of distractions: a place where I could deal with my grief and try to recover from it.

My artwork changed dramatically. Mirroring my subconscious emotions, darker colors and images began to emerge as I poured my anguish into my creations: a solitary sunflower plant drooping in a desolate winter field, a leafless oak tree silhouetted on a bleak horizon, a macabre sketch of road kill—all executed in somber tones of black and gray. The images were wrenching to create and disturbing to look at, but they helped me express my grief and emptiness and work my way out of my depression. They were my salvation.

Along with a miraculous intervention.

A month or so into the summer following my junior year, my art teacher, Ms. MacLerren, contacted Pop to ask if I'd like to visit her in New York City for a couple of weeks. She went there every summer, after high school classes ended, to study at the Art Students League. She figured I needed a break from the memory of Matthew's death. She also thought I should begin thinking about where to go to art school after

I graduated. She thought it might be helpful for me to see New York City and see what classes at the League were like.

She was right. As soon as I sat in on one of her classes, I knew the school was the place I needed to be—and we began making plans for me to apply to its program in Fine Arts Painting after my senior year.

As my future began to take shape and my broken heart slowly healed, I remembered what an old family friend, Mr. M, had told me years before, when I was a scared little girl trying to cope with my mother's death: "Making art," he had said, "can save you."

Lessons

I HAD JUST ARRIVED IN NEW YORK CITY, an eighteen-year-old farm girl from the Missouri Ozarks ready to begin art school at the prestigious Art Students League. It was the most exciting time of my young life—and the most terrifying.

New York was the international capital of the art world, a city filled with museums and galleries and prominent artists. And the Art Students League, or ASL, was one of the premier art schools in the country, boasting a faculty made up of influential, cutting-edge art instructors. Did I really belong there? Did I have enough talent to compete with ambitious, accomplished students from all over America?

Along with those crippling self-doubts, I was also scared stiff that I might disappoint my patron back home in Plainfield—Mr. M, the old family friend who, astonishingly, had not only volunteered to pay my tuition and lodging expenses in New York but had insisted upon it. "Hallie's been like a daughter to me," he told my father. "The child I never had. For years, I've been putting money away for her to go to art school."

At first, Pop wouldn't hear of it. "Doris and I planned for this. It's already covered."

But Mr. M was unshakable. No matter what argument Pop threw at him, there was no talking him out of my *not* attending the art school of my choice and his *not* covering the costs. It *would* happen, and we'd just have to accept his generosity. "You've got to let me do this," Mr. M persisted. "This is what money's for, and this is how I want to spend it."

Eventually he wore my father down. But now I had to live up to the trust our dear friend was placing in me. Was I really good enough?

"Of course you are," I kept telling myself. After all, I'd been accepted into the ASL's full-time four-year program in Fine Arts Painting, so I figured I must have at least some talent and potential. But I also knew it would be up to me to succeed in my studies and in my new life in the big city.

"New York City couldn't be more different from Plainfield," Pop fretted. "And you won't have Madelyn MacLerren to advise you or protect you. You'll be on your own, and you'll have to deal with everything life throws at you."

For starters, I—a small, unassuming teenaged girl on my own for the first time—had to face the crush of humanity that seemed to swallow me up the minute I stepped onto the city's streets. There were hordes of people everywhere, moving purposefully and paying no attention to me. I felt as if they could—and would—walk over me if I hesitated for a split second. It didn't take long for me to learn to move briskly to avoid being bumped into or pushed aside.

"Or worse," Ms. MacLerren, my high school art teacher, had warned me. "You might have your purse snatched or your wallet stolen. Or you might be grabbed at or even mugged." I was appalled, but she continued with her advice. "And never look anybody—particularly men—in the eye. They might think you *want* them." She said this in a way that even I, a naïve country girl, understood.

It was a lesson I quickly learned when, inadvertently, I locked eyes with a disheveled-looking man on the subway who engaged me in conversation, then began pressuring me to come home with him.

When they heard about the incident, my new housemates, Adrianna and Carla, told me to keep my head up, look serious, and walk assertively. "If you look like you mean business and know what you're doing and will cause trouble for anybody who bothers you, you'll pretty much be left alone."

I'd been fortunate to find my two housemates and the apartment that would be my new home. Since the Art Students League offered no housing accommodations, students were on their own to find a place to live. As soon as I arrived in New York, I checked the ASL bulletin board for suitable lodgings and jumped on the advertisement that Adrianna and Carla had posted—particularly since the place was in a safe neighborhood only three subway stops from the ASL building.

The apartment was a loft that had been carved into three bedrooms with a small but fully functioning kitchen and bathroom. The bedrooms were tiny, but each one had a small window to let some light and air in and was outfitted with an unusual sleeping contraption with a bunk bed on top and a large, wide chest of drawers below. A workspace consisting of a tabletop placed on a pair of file cabinets took up a good part of the opposite wall.

Adrianna was in her third year of studies at the Art Students League and Carla, her second, so they knew the ropes about the school and the city.

Everything about my life in New York was so new and different that I felt like a foreigner. But I didn't dare let on. I was determined to shed my country image and fit into the city's art scene and not reveal my inexperience and naïveté. The last thing in the world I wanted to do was come off as a small town hick. So I followed whatever advice my housemates offered and tried to fit into the alien world I'd been dropped into.

And what a world it was! It was 1969, and the times and guidelines for acceptable behavior were changing, in ways I could never have imagined. My new environment was wild and scary but also exhilarating, because I now had the freedom to do whatever I wanted.

It was also the era of free love—so different from what I'd always imagined being intimate with another person would be. Rather than make love with one special person you'd dated for a while and had grown to trust, girls now had spontaneous, straightforward sex, whenever, wherever, and with whomever they liked.

"You mean you're still a virgin?" Carla asked me shortly after I moved in. "Well," she chuckled, "that won't last long. But just make sure you've got protection." The next day, she took me to a neighborhood clinic where I was examined and given birth-control pills. Welcome, Hallie Jo Everheart, to the liberated new world of the late sixties.

My first sexual encounter was with Roddy, a first-year student in one of my art classes. We'd gone to a nearby café for coffee. He offered me a cigarette, which I immediately declined. But right away, I noticed that almost everyone else there was smoking. That night, I bummed a cigarette from Carla and watched how she did it—standing so coolly and confidently, inhaling deeply and blowing smoke out an open window. The next time Roddy offered me a cigarette, I took it.

Then, one afternoon, a couple of weeks later, we walked to Central Park, where in an out-of-the-way bower Roddy introduced me to marijuana. "Pot," he called it. It burned my lungs and made me cough when I tried it. He laughed, then told me to inhale the smoke slowly and hold it in as long as I could. After a couple of tries, I had an odd, floating feeling that was strange but not unpleasant. Then Roddy laid me down, and I lost my virginity. It wasn't bad, and it wasn't good—just different from what I'd expected. After that, I had relations with him again and eventually with a couple of other ASL boys. Carla said that if a guy was attractive,

I shouldn't say no—that I was so green I needed all the experience I could get. And, though I wasn't promiscuous—and felt uneasy about every encounter, as if I was somehow letting my father down—I went along with what seemed to be normal behavior. Anything to fit in; besides, it was flattering to be desired.

My roommates and I lived on soups and stews, spaghetti, rice and beans, and ramen noodles. We slapped together bologna sandwiches and peanut butter and jelly on day-old bread from a nearby bakery and ate street food on the run. Sometimes Carla seemed to be living entirely on cigarettes and coffee. "Can't be too thin or have too many lovers," she'd say, looking increasingly haggard as the weeks went by.

I never took to the city's night life the way my housemates did. Though going to the gritty live-music clubs was exciting, I always felt a little frightened in them. But I loved dancing and quickly picked up the latest moves, giving myself up to the pounding beat of the rock music. Drinking was another matter. Unfortunately, I'd become sleepy after a glass or two of wine and would wake up the next morning feeling ragged and disoriented. "You'll get used to it," Adrianna predicted.

What I took to most of all was the New York City art scene. After classes and on the weekends, my roommates and I spent our time visiting the collections of the city's world-class art museums—the Metropolitan, MoMA, the Guggenheim, the Whitney, and the National Academy of Design—or checking out the trendiest new exhibitions in New York's countless commercial galleries. For an aspiring young artist, it was all there: classic masterworks in the museums, the latest, most innovative cutting-edge work in the galleries.

But most of my life revolved around my art classes—classes in composition and drawing, artistic anatomy, mixed media, watercolor, landscape and still-life painting, "life painting" with nude models, and portraiture—taught by an impressive array of brilliant instructors, each an accomplished artist in his or her own right. The faculty spanned the spectrum of twentieth-century art movements—social realism, abstract expressionism, classical portraiture, minimalism, Old Master-style realism, and more. Whatever approach to art you were interested in, there was a prominent instructor to teach it to you. To the students, the instructors were gods and their studios hallowed ground.

One instructor in particular—Andreas Richter—gradually began to take a special interest in me. Richter was a handsome, forty-something Czech émigré with long hair, a thick accent, and a suave European persona. A specialist in a minimalist form of classical realism reminiscent of Georgia O'Keeffe's early work, he had exhibited in several one-man shows at private New York galleries, receiving flattering reviews from the city's art critics. He had taught at ASL for more than a decade and was one of the most highly regarded members of the faculty.

Richter's classes were popular and always inspiring. "You must learn how to see! How to feel!" he would bellow. "Figure out why a subject moves you, why it speaks to you." When making a point, he would nod so vigorously that a lock of his shaggy hair would fall onto his forehead. He'd sweep it from his face with a dramatic gesture and go on. "Ask yourself: what is it about the subject that most needs to be expressed?"

He had a reputation for resting his hands on the shoulders of his female students while he was evaluating their work-in-progress. He would physically guide their fingers when demonstrating brush strokes or shading techniques. Many of his female students had a crush on him.

During my first two years at ASL, I took a couple of courses with him. Though his teaching style was a little too familiar and "touchy-feely" for my comfort, I had tried not to flinch when he put his hands on me while he was evaluating my painting. It wasn't until my third year that events happened that would drastically change my life.

During my third course with him, he began flattering me with praise, telling me my work was very good—"unusual," "intriguing"—which pleased me no end. "But you're too tense," he informed me one day as he stood behind me massaging my shoulders and neck with both hands. "You'll never become a real artist if you don't loosen up." I was mortified, but thankfully none of the other students around me seemed to be paying any attention. "You've got potential," he went on. "But you've *got* to learn how to let go of your inhibitions and express your inner impulses more freely."

What in the world was he talking about? I went to clubs with my friends and danced all night. I wasn't afraid to smoke or drink. Occasionally, I smoked pot and had sex with a boyfriend. I already *knew* how to be loose and free. But I was also a serious artist who never missed classes and always carried a sketchbook. I drew constantly, trying to capture as precisely as possible whatever sparked my imagination. Though I was naturally flattered and encouraged by Richter's praise, I didn't understand what he meant about needing to be less tense. I didn't realize that I was being groomed.

One Saturday night, he hosted a get-together for some of his students in his combination apartment and studio in Greenwich Village. There was plenty of good wine and food, lively conversation about art, the Vietnam War, and anything else that happened to interest him. We sat rapt, absorbing his words and opinions like holy scripture. For many of us, he was like royalty, a man to be listened to and treated with deference.

As the party wound down, he whispered to me that he wanted me to stay after the others left. He had something to discuss with me. I presumed it was about a project I'd been working on in class and felt honored that he would single me out for attention. He showed me to a chair near a work table in his studio—a space partitioned from his living quarters—then left the room, leaving me to take in all that surrounded me: tubes of paint, jars of solvents, pencils, charcoal, sketchbooks, cans of brushes, and other paraphernalia. Various works-in-progress were displayed upon sturdy easels scattered around the room, with rolls of canvas leaning against a lopsided bookcase crammed with catalogs, periodicals, and books.

He returned with coffee. I needed it, because I'd had too much wine and was becoming sleepy.

"Tell me about yourself," he said, settling into a chair close beside me.

"There's not much to tell," I mumbled.

"I think there is," he said, looking at me intently. "What do you like? What do you want to do with your life? Your art?"

No one at school had ever taken this much interest in me—much less an instructor as esteemed as Andreas Richter. I needed a moment to order my thoughts and figure out what to say.

He bored in. "You're serious, reserved. Sometimes you seem almost sad." He reached out and tapped my head with his fingertips. "What's going on up there? What makes you tick?"

I found my voice and started in. "First of all, I'm determined to become the best artist I can be. I love my classes, and I'm learning so much."

"But . . . ?"

"But sometimes I get homesick."

"Where's home?"

"Plainfield, Missouri, a small town in the Ozark Mountains where I grew up."

"That's a long way from New York City, geographically and culturally."

"Tell me about it," I replied. "A lot of the time I feel like a fish out of water here."

"That explains a lot," he said under his breath.

Afraid that I might have offended him, I hastened to add, "The city's exciting and there's so much to see and do. And loads of opportunity. I've had experiences beyond my wildest imaginings. I'm grateful to be here."

"But . . . ?"

"But everything moves so fast here! A lot of the time, I can barely take it all in or think clearly and calmly and quietly enough to decide what it is I really want to do."

Richter sighed. "The ASL's programs are intense, and they can sometimes feel a little overwhelming. But you'll get the tools here—damn good tools—to do serious work, work that's yours and yours alone." He took my hand. "When you approach the canvas, what is it that inspires you the most?" He looked as if nothing in the world mattered more to him than what I was about to say.

I felt shy. Here I was about to bare my soul to someone I barely knew. Would he think I was stupid? Frivolous? Unworthy of further attention? I swallowed my fear, then said, "Well, Mr. Richter, I've always wanted to capture the inner spirits of things. Their souls. I'm trying to do that in my painting, but I'm not there yet. I want to know more, do more, do it better."

"Please, Hallie, call me Andy—not Mr. Richter. And don't worry. You'll know more and do better by doing more. And by looking even more closely at things—at what they're made up of. Mentally x-ray your subjects until you can see inside them, until you know every muscle and bone and inner part. Whether it's an object, a landscape, a person, or something else, find its inner light. Feel its living energy. Then draw it, and draw it some more. Draw it as fully as you can from different angles and in different lighting."

His words thrilled me. "Remember, your instructors can only take you so far. You've got to get all you can out of your classes, but after that, you have to unleash your own creative genius. And some of the best advice I can give you is to experience life! Take risks! Don't be afraid of making mistakes! In the process, you'll learn to trust the way you see, trust the way you feel, and trust your own judgment." He took my hand and said, "You need to define your technique more specifically. You say that you want to capture the inner spirits of your subjects. But what kind of subjects are you most drawn to? What medium works best for you? What color palette?" He reached up and caressed my cheek. "Tell me what burns inside you—what you yearn to create. I know I can help you."

I was so overcome with excitement that I could hardly breathe. When I could finally speak, it was as if a dam had broken loose inside me, and all my pent-up homesickness came pouring out. "I can't help but think about the Ozarks," I said. "No matter how I try to block it out, I think and dream about my life back there: the trees and trucks and barns and gardens; the hills rising behind our fields; the lone tree at the edge of the cornfield; a nest in our henhouse with two perfect brown eggs; overalls hanging on the clothesline. I try to put all these images out of my mind, but they continue to haunt me."

"Why put them out of your mind?"

"I'm in New York City. I should be focusing on important subjects. I mean, why am I here, otherwise?"

"You know why you're here: to get the tools and experience you need to become the best artist you can be. But there's no reason why you shouldn't focus your creative energy on the thing you're most drawn to—and that sounds like these Ozarks you're talking about. What you need to do is decide which painting technique allows you to capture their inner spirit most effectively. Right now, Abstract Expressionism is on the way out, and we're moving into true Minimalism and Pop Art. But even though you may appreciate some of this modern stuff, it doesn't sound like it's suited to what you want to do."

"What do you suggest?"

He paused in thought for a moment. "Have you ever looked at Andrew Wyeth's work?"

"I've seen it, but I haven't paid much attention to it."

"He's considered a regionalist painter. He paints the objects and people and countryside of the two places where he lives: rural Pennsylvania and coastal Maine. Although his work is out-of-fashion right now—considered passé by avant-garde artists and critics and snubbed by many of them—you really ought to look at it."

Over the next few days, I went to the Met and MoMA and the National Academy of Design to look in detail at Wyeth's works. I also spent several hours in the ASL library reading everything I could about him. The following Saturday afternoon, I returned to Richter's studio. "Well?" he asked.

"I can't believe it!" I burst out. "He sees things the way I do; he draws and paints the types of things I want to. And in the colors I want to use."

"What else did you notice?"

"On the surface of things, his work seems so spare and simple. But it's not simple at all; it's layered with life and meaning. He seems to be able to capture the inner lives of things, just the way I want to."

"Good. But what else?"

"His painting has an edge to it—each piece seems to pulse with some strange kind of under-life. His images are so stark, so uncompromising, so brutally direct and honest—and they tell a story."

"And what else?"

"Well, for all its starkness, his work also seems so harmonious. He's a master at capturing the essence of peoples' lives and their place in the rural landscapes around them." Richter nodded in encouragement. "And the colors he uses convey the atmospheres he's trying to capture—tones I'd love to use in my own work. What does he use to get them?"

"Much of his painting is done in egg tempera, a medium that, to a great extent, stopped being used once oils were developed and refined. It's a technique where the artist mixes egg yolk with paint. It's more complicated than other mediums. But, as you've noticed, it produces a distinctive look: those soft, dry, understated tones that seem to appeal to you. I've experimented with it, occasionally. When you're ready, I'll show you how to do it."

He invited me to come back the following weekend. "You need a quiet place away from city life and city concerns—someplace where you can experiment without all the distractions."

"What do I need to do?"

"Come here to my studio every Saturday—late afternoons—and I'll work with you."

"But what'll I tell my housemates? And won't other students complain that I'm getting special treatment?"

"Tell them you've got a grant for the upcoming year to be my assistant, helping me mix paints, stretch canvases, straighten up, and other things. It'll be like an apprenticeship where you help me and I help you. It's a fairly common practice." He smiled warmly and intimately. "Along with the art, we'll work on getting you loosened up. But you'll need to do whatever I say."

When I showed up at his studio the following Saturday, the first thing he had me do was draw some of the Ozark images that were lodged inside my mind. "Draw the things that mean something to you!" he said. "Draw what you relate to! Draw your life!"

He also had me study Wyeth's techniques in greater detail. "When you look at one of his paintings, ask yourself why he chose that particular subject and color palette, why he used that particular perspective. You need to approach your work in the same way. Even more importantly, you need to ask yourself what your subject is saying to you as well as what you're trying to say about it. What's its story? Its inner life?"

For the next four weeks, I thought intensely about these questions, trying to answer them in my compositions. Richter—Andy—set up a table for me in a corner of his studio and frequently came by to look over my shoulder and show me tricks that helped make my subjects become more real, more alive.

Soon, however, it became clear that he had other techniques in mind as well.

While I was working in the studio one afternoon, he began to knead my shoulders sensually. "You're too uptight," he said. "You need to loosen up before you can become the artist you want to be."

The following Saturday he was more direct. "Take your shirt off. I need to have direct access to your muscles."

Midway through our next meeting—while I was leaning over the table to lay out a series of sketches for a formal drawing—he began feeling my hips. When he tried to turn me around, I resisted, but I was no match for him. Seeing that I was frightened, he backed off, circling around me and looking at me from every angle. "You'll never become a real artist until you learn to relax," he said for what seemed to be the nth time. "And I suppose I'll have to show you how to do that, too."

He told me to take off my jeans. When I hesitated, he said pointedly, "Do you want to become a real artist or not?"

He guided me to a straight-backed chair. "Sit," he said and began rubbing my legs, first below the knees, then my thighs. Then higher. . . and higher.

"Take off your panties," he instructed. "You need to be completely free." I seized up, hoping I hadn't heard correctly, but he was serious. "What's it going to take to get you to relax?" he asked. "You'll never develop your creative skills like this."

My mind was a blur of confusion. "Should I be doing this? But if I don't, will he get angry and throw me out of the studio—maybe tell the other instructors I'm no good and they shouldn't bother to work with me?"

I'd always heard that artists had to make sacrifices to achieve their goals. Talent, by itself, wasn't enough. Maybe this was one of the sacrifices I needed to make to realize my dream.

And, I reminded myself, Richter was a prominent instructor who'd singled me out for special attention. He cared about me. He was a professional. He knew what needed to be done. Even if parts of his plan didn't seem quite right, I needed to trust him and do what he said. He was the master craftsman. I was the apprentice.

I removed my panties, and he laid me down on top of his bed. "It's the best way to get you fully relaxed," he insisted.

I didn't say a word and did as he said.

"You do want to do good work, don't you?" he asked as he massaged my abdomen. "Remember, your body is a conduit." He was silent for a few minutes, studying my naked body and focusing his attention on my thick bush of reddish-blond pubic hair. "I wouldn't waste my time on you if I didn't think you have potential."

He stopped rubbing my belly and began expertly massaging the most sensitive part of my sex organ, continuing until I experienced the most intense fluttery sensation—as if I was detached from the world and flying free. Though I'd masturbated alone in my room a few times, this was the first orgasm I'd ever had with a man.

"Now that I've gotten you opened up that way, we can really get down to business," I heard him murmur.

The following week, he penetrated me vaginally.

And a weekly pattern began. Before we started working on our art, we had to "loosen up." We'd both have orgasms, after which we'd go into the studio and work. After I got over my initial reticence and embarrassment, I grew to enjoy— maybe even depend on—this weekly release, and felt special because he'd chosen me.

"Tell me about your sexual exploits," he asked one day.

"What exploits?" I replied. "I've only had sex with a couple of guys—and, compared to you, they didn't know what they were doing."

My answer seemed to please him immensely. "You're showing signs of becoming a wonderful artist," he told me again and again. "And getting better all the time. And more relaxed. But we still have plenty of work to do."

And work we did. Along with assisting him, he gave me free use of his art materials and studio space, and his individual instruction was invaluable. "Paint what you know and feel most deeply and intimately," he advised.

Back at my apartment I unearthed an old high school sketchbook I'd brought with me to New York from home. It was filled with crude sketches and Polaroid snapshots of local subjects in and around Plainfield that I'd thought were interesting—part of a senior-year assignment from Ms. MacLerren. When I showed Andy a rough sketch I'd made of an old wooden plow leaning against the weathered boards of an unpainted barn on our family farm, he encouraged me to try to develop it more fully in a Wyeth style using tempera, which he showed me how to mix using a combination of egg yolks, white vinegar, paint, and distilled water. The painting that resulted was, in Andy's words, "rather original" and "very promising."

Soon I was using the old sketches and photos to produce a whole series of Ozark-based tempera paintings—a farmhouse at sunset, sacks of grain piled symmetrically on the loading ramp of a farm-supply store, a rusted old pickup truck parked in front of a glitzy five-and-dime on Main Street, a bird's-eye view of an abandoned Baptist church disappearing in a field of scrub brush and high weeds, the Plainfield water tower with an electrical storm approaching in the sky behind it— paintings done in the muted, naturalistic brown and gray hues favored by Wyeth, paintings that in their small way seemed to express something about the "soul" of the rural Ozark landscape and culture. They were good—and other ASL instructors I showed them to agreed.

The next several months were a blur of artistic productivity as I poured myself into my newfound genre.

And then my twenty-first birthday arrived. "I've got a special birthday surprise for you," Andy announced when I entered the studio that afternoon. We worked in the studio without preliminary "loosening up," then paused for a supper of soup and sandwiches delivered by a local deli. He uncorked a bottle of expensive, very dry champagne and toasted my coming of age and the progress I was making as a painter. We talked for hours, finishing the champagne. Before I knew it, I was tipsy.

"Now try this," he said, placing a tiny tab of something on my tongue. Within minutes, I felt like I'd entered a radically different universe. Colors were suddenly more vibrant than ever before—swirling and pulsating—communicating to me in an unknown language, but one I intuitively could grasp.

I felt alive at a new level—every pore of me. My blood and brain began vibrating to the beat of the colors. I understood so much about . . . well . . . everything: art, the world, the universe, and beyond. I was only vaguely aware of Andreas Richter holding me, caressing me, and probing me—turning me this way and that in new and different positions.

I felt a sensation of overpowering pressure, then a stab of pain that continued until I thought I couldn't bear it anymore, which soon moderated into a flood of warmth that offered some relief from the pain as well as a partial release of the pressure. The lower part of my body throbbed and felt oddly distended—in some way stretched out of shape—while the rest of my being continued to keep time to the rhythmic beat of the swirling colors, which eventually turned dark, then darker and darker still.

When I woke up, it was almost dawn, and I was lying on a sofa in the studio under an old army blanket. My clothes were folded in a pile nearby. Everything looked vague and slightly distorted. My head throbbed, and I was sore all over. I groaned when I sat up and attempted to stretch the kinks out of my body. Richter came into the room and handed me a cup of coffee. "Drink this. You'll feel better," he said.

"What happened? Where am I?"

"You passed out and spent the night here with me."

"Here?" I felt queasy.

"Don't worry. You're fine."

"But I've got to get home! What will my housemates think?"

Richter chuckled. "I doubt if they'll even notice. And if they do, just say that you were too drunk to make it home."

"But what happened?"

"I gave you some acid—just a speck as a special birthday present. I guess you've never had it before. It really expands the consciousness!"

"I feel dizzy, and I ache all over."

"You'll get over it."

"I'd better get home." I reached for my clothes and struggled to put them on: the buttons wouldn't line up and the zippers wouldn't zip.

I felt disconnected from my surroundings as I made my way back to my apartment. To my relief, my housemates were still asleep when I got there. I retreated to my bedroom, where I collapsed on my bed.

Sometime later, I awoke to the smell of coffee. When I sat up in bed, I discovered that my backside was horribly sore. There were dried blood stains on the back part of my panties, and my rear end felt as if it'd been ripped apart.

I'd heard about anal intercourse, but I never thought I would experience it—and certainly not without my knowledge or consent. Surely Andy wouldn't—couldn't—have done that to me.

But he had. "Happy Birthday," he'd told me as I was leaving to return to my apartment. "Now you're completely opened up."

At first, I was confused and bewildered, even ashamed—as if I'd done something to encourage this physical abuse. I also felt violated, tricked, betrayed.

But I couldn't allow any of this to stop me from working on my art projects or going to class.

When I arrived at Andy's studio the following weekend, I could hardly look at him. When he tried to touch me, I pushed him off, saying I was too sore. How long this excuse would work, I had no idea. There were three more Saturdays left before the end of the school year, so I'd have to think of something. And I needed to concentrate on completing my last drawings and paintings before classes let out.

The next time I went to his studio, I begged off having any sort of intercourse, saying I was still too sore.

At first, he said nothing about what had happened. When he finally did bring it up, it was indirectly. "You needed to be loosened up all the way," he insisted. "You needed to be brought in touch with *all* of your sexuality, so you can put it into your work." When I looked at him skeptically, he added, "Painting's not for the weak or timid. It takes strength and spirit and uninhibited passion. You need to *feel* your subjects, *know* them, make *love* to them—even if it's only an old truck or a tree. You need to penetrate their inner depths."

I must have looked grim, for he went on to declare self-righteously, "I've now opened you up to life and have given you all I could—all you needed."

"And more," I said dryly.

"I don't think so," he snorted. "In time, you'll realize that there was more to all this than my own selfish desire."

The days flew by until the end of the school year arrived, and with it, the end of my time with Andreas Richter.

Then it was June, and Andy took off to spend the summer in an arts community in New Hampshire. I caught a flight back to Missouri to spend a few days in Plainfield to get my bearings and accumulate more ideas and photos for Ozark paintings. Then I'd drive back to New York with Ms. MacLerren for our usual round of summer courses at ASL.

"So how was your year?" she asked as soon as we got on the road.

"Fine," I said.

"Fine?"

"Yeah, I learned a lot."

"That doesn't tell me very much. What did you do? Who did you work with?"

"Mostly Andreas Richter. I did an informal apprenticeship with him."

"Oh?" There was an odd tone in her voice. "And how did that work out?" She didn't wait for my answer before adding, "Some of us have had problems with him. His manners and methods are, shall we say, 'unorthodox.'"

"'Unorthodox' is one way of describing it," I said without looking at her.

She sighed. "Oh, dear. I should have warned you about him. He's something of a womanizer—and likes to recruit attractive female students to be his 'assistants.'"

I smiled grimly.

Ms. MacLerren sighed again. "And given his stature at the League, there's not much anybody can do about it."

"Yeah. Who'd believe the truth?"

"What happened?"

I told her all of it, sparing no details. "I got an education, all right," I concluded.

"That bastard!" she hissed.

"For a while, I thought maybe I'd done something to cause it."

"No, he raped you, pure and simple!"

To hear the bare-bones truth shocked me so much I couldn't say a word. I sat quietly, listening to the hum of the motor and trying to force back a wave of shame and despair.

"Still, with your trusting nature and your inexperience with men, something like this was probably bound to happen. But he didn't have to rape you!"

"It's something I'll never forget."

I didn't want to dwell on the incident, so to move past it, I took a deep breath and announced, "Well, at least I *did* get something positive from working with him." Ms. MacLerren looked skeptical, but I went on. "I now have a much better idea of what style of painting I want to concentrate on."

"Oh?"

"Andy suggested that I look at Andrew Wyeth's work. So I did, and it turned out to be a form of painting that really speaks to me. He also showed me how to use egg tempera to get the Wyeth-style effects I want."

I went on to explain that during my time in New York City I'd found that I kept returning in my mind to the Ozarks—that I couldn't get them out of my system. "I've come to realize that my real inspiration as an artist comes from right at home in Plainfield—its local landscapes and buildings and people and colors and rhythms of life. If I paint them right, they speak to something basic, something essential and true about the rural Midwest, about its cultural environment and the lives of its people."

"More power to you," Ms. MacLerren responded. "I can't say I'm surprised, but I'm just so proud of you!" There was a look of quiet appreciation and satisfaction on her face.

The summer sped by and suddenly it was time for Ms. MacLerren to pack up and return to Plainfield while I prepared for my final year of courses. As I did so, I was aware that in many ways I was a different person than I had been when I arrived in the city three years earlier. I'd learned some important lessons about life, and about the life I wanted to live.

I'd learned, first of all, that I needed to be more guarded in my relationships with men—that I needed to keep my elbows up and not be so naïve and vulnerable.

I had also come to realize that I had the talent to be a serious artist, perhaps not at the level of an Andrew Wyeth or a Georgia O'Keeffe, but an artist who could portray the world she came from in fresh, original, maybe even insightful, ways.

And above all, I'd learned that New York City was an alien world to me and I didn't belong there—that I belonged back in the Ozarks where I could feel at home and nurture my creative impulses surrounded by a lifetime's worth of inspiration.

Although I hadn't been fully aware of it as it was happening, I'd undergone an important transformation during my years in New York City—a transformation from girlhood to womanhood.

Lost and Found

I HAD JUST COMPLETED MY FOURTH AND FINAL YEAR of courses at the Art Students League—ASL—in New York City and was packing my things for the move back home to Missouri, with no idea what I was going to do next, when the phone rang. It was my high school art teacher, friend, and adviser, Madelyn MacLerren. From the subdued and halting tone of her voice, I could sense that I was about to hear some very bad news.

She had just been diagnosed with stage-four breast cancer and was heading to the Barnes-Jewish Hospital in St. Louis for intensive chemotherapy. By this time, she'd been living and teaching in Plainfield for close to a decade, although unbeknownst to her colleagues and students she had recently been trying to find a way to relocate to St. Louis to live closer to her aging parents. She'd managed to land a teaching job as an art instructor at the Woodbury Academy, a private secondary school outside St. Louis, beginning the following month, but had just informed the principal of the academy that her medical situation would prevent her from fulfilling her contract. Desperate to fill the instructional vacancy with no time left for a formal search, the principal had agreed to consider her recommendation that—based on my rigorous training and exemplary work at the prestigious ASL—I fill in for her on a temporary emergency basis. Was I interested? And if so, would it be all right if he called ASL to confirm my credentials?

A week later, after a long phone interview with the principal (and strong recommendations from several ASL instructors, including faculty luminary Andreas Richter), I was hired.

My God! I'd only just finished my coursework at ASL and had no teaching experience other than occasionally filling in for a couple of the art school instructors teaching children's courses in the summer or on weekends. How in the world would I ever be able to teach high school students—at a private academy, no less?

And at only twenty-two years of age, I'd be barely older than my students. Would they respect me? Listen to me? Do what I asked of them in class? Despite my nervousness, I knew I wouldn't dare to display any weakness or uncertainty in front of them.

"Just be yourself," Ms. MacLerren advised. "Teach what you know, and remember that you do know quite a bit—a lot more than the students. This job will give you valuable experience and credentials that could be very useful to you down the road."

The ensuing year was a blur, as—with Ms. MacLerren's help along with advice from ASL instructors with whom I had worked—I frantically put together lesson plans, usually the night before the following day's classes.

I also relied heavily on my memory of the classes I'd taken with Ms. MacLerren at Plainfield High, especially the way she presented herself. I updated my wardrobe to look more polished and professional and tried to emulate her confident, professional demeanor.

Though I was afraid of making a fool of myself in class, I managed to stay calm whenever something unfamiliar came up and was able to laugh at myself when I committed some embarrassing blunder, like when in my haste to rinse my brush, I knocked an entire glass of watercolor water onto the floor, or when my arm and shoulder brushed against the series of charcoal sketches I'd been drawing to demonstrate techniques, ruining both the sketches and my blouse. From the start, I also adopted an attitude of openness with the students, letting them know that "we're all in this together, learning together."

And we were. Though every lesson was a reiteration of what I'd learned in high school or at ASL, I enjoyed the challenge of coming up with new ways of applying basic concepts and techniques that might pique the students' interest and further their development. I encouraged them to use their imaginations and pursue what might seem like unusual subjects for their sketches: over-sized insects, exotic invented creatures, or mundane objects rendered in psychedelic colors. No subject was too wild to consider. To get them going, I brought in props like a pair of exuberantly flowered bell-bottoms, a beat-up tin coffee pot, and odd-looking tools and utensils.

By the time the exhausting school year came to an end, I felt confident that I'd given the students and the academy their money's worth. My temporary contract had come to an end, however, and, as I had expected, the school's principal decided to hire someone with more experience and credentials. The worst period of my life was about to begin.

I was out of a job, with no real prospects or any ideas about what I would do next, other than work on my painting. And then, without warning, people I loved began dying around me—three in the space of two-and-a-half months.

In late June, two weeks after my teaching position ended, Ms. MacLerren succumbed to breast cancer in her St. Louis hospital. I'd been so busy with end-of-the-school-year responsibilities that I hadn't visited her in several weeks and never had a chance to tell her how much she meant to me.

A month later, as I reeled from the loss of my mentor and friend, tragedy struck again. Early on a rainy, humid Missouri morning, my stepmother, Doris, called to tell me that Pop had had a sudden heart attack and died without regaining consciousness.

In a stupor of grief and disbelief, I packed my bags and raced back to Plainfield. How could this be? Pop had seemed to be in perfect health. At fifty-eight, he was as strong and vigorous as ever and showed no signs of slowing down. With the farm now making a decent profit, the future looked bright. Pop was happy, content, and looking forward to a good long life with Doris and her boys—Mark, eighteen and soon going off to college, and the twins, Luke and John, two years younger.

Pop always said that bad things usually come in threes, and this was no exception, because five weeks later Mr. M—our old family friend and my beloved benefactor and advisor—had a massive stroke and died at age seventy-five.

I felt like the bottom had dropped out of my world, and I entered a period of uncontrolled emotional free fall. I knew that people died; it was the natural order of things. But usually the deaths of your loved ones didn't all happen at once. I had just barely become an adult, and three of the people who meant the most to me in the world were suddenly gone. Their loss, concentrated in such a short period of time, was psychologically crippling and left me in a state of numbed grief. It was as if a void had opened up inside me. I missed them so badly that I could barely function. For the first time in my life, I felt utterly alone in the world.

In my grief and despair, I prayed with all my might for the fortitude to go on with my life without the support of the three people I most depended on—to not only survive their loss but find the strength to help Doris and my three stepbrothers keep our farm going, the farm we depended on for our economic survival.

I was struggling to keep myself together when the day of Mr. M's funeral arrived, and suddenly out of this intense series of crushing losses came a new beginning.

I'd been so grief-stricken during the funeral service that I hadn't paid much attention to the eulogizing—much less to who was there. Afterwards, at a reception held in Mr. M's farmhouse, I'd been too distraught to mingle with the guests and had stolen away into his living room, a place I was intimately familiar with from the age of nine.

Alone in the room, I struggled to keep my emotions under control. As I walked around, looking at familiar objects that held deep memories for me, I noticed that the grandfather clock had fallen silent. A new wave of grief and loss swept over me. As long as there'd been breath in his body, Mr. M had religiously kept that clock wound up and ticking. Suddenly, I felt that by getting it re-started, I would somehow be paying homage to his memory.

As I was rewinding the clock, a boy who appeared to be nine or ten years old ambled into the room. Tall and wiry— all arms and legs—he had a coltish look to him. He stared at me with an inquisitive expression and asked, "What're you doing?"

"I'm winding the clock," I replied. "Mr. M always kept it going."

"Mr. M?"

"That's my private name for Mr. Morrison."

"That's my great-great uncle," the boy informed me.

I didn't have time to respond before we heard a voice calling, "Jared? Jared?" A pleasant-looking man in his mid-thirties paused in the doorway, then entered the room. He had the look of the young big-city professional about him: clean-shaven, but with fashionably long sandy brown hair, and dressed in khakis, a blue blazer, and a trendy muted-plaid sport shirt with a solid color-coordinated tie. His wire-rim glasses added a bit of a hip aspect to his appearance. Not the type of man you ran into very often in Plainfield.

The boy turned to him. "Dad, she calls Uncle Jared 'Mr. M.'" The man turned to me, curiosity wrinkling his brow. "You do?"

"When I first met your uncle, I was a little girl and his full name was too much of a mouthful for me to say. So I made up a shorter name—a special one nobody else used." I smiled at the memory. "He really liked it."

"I like it, too," Jared murmured.

With that, we all introduced ourselves. Jared's father was named Micah Morrison. "So you've known Uncle Jared a long time?"

"Not as long as you have," I replied.

"Actually, we haven't." He explained that throughout his life, he'd been vaguely aware of the existence of a great uncle somewhere. Then, out of the blue, Micah's father, Henry Morrison, had been notified by a Plainfield attorney that he'd inherited his uncle's estate. Shaken by Pop's death, Mr. M had recently put his affairs in order, and in his updated will he had decided to leave his estate—including his Plainfield farm—to his nephew, Henry. It'd all taken place so suddenly that Henry didn't yet know what he was going to do with his inheritance, and because he had a demanding position in state government in St. Louis, he didn't have time to deal with it at the moment. As a result, Micah, his son, had agreed to come down to Plainfield and sort things out.

"So you may be seeing quite a bit of Jared and me," Micah said, smiling as he loosened his tie. "For a while, we're going to be down here every weekend or so."

"Please let me know if there's anything I can do to help," I told them. I said I'd be happy to drive out to Mr. M's farm a couple of times a week to meet with the supervisor of his work crew—who for decades had tended Mr. M's orchards and hives and pressed cider from his apples—to answer any questions or relay messages.

The weekend following the funeral, I went out to the farm to update Micah on the week's developments. Since the work crew knew what needed to be done without much direction, the place seemed to be running smoothly for the time being.

This gave me an opportunity to get to know Micah and Jared better.

"I can't believe he's gone!" I moaned one afternoon as we all were sitting at Mr. M's kitchen table, sipping freshly pressed cider.

"I can't believe I never met him!" Micah responded. "I don't know anything about him!"

"That's not too surprising. Your uncle was a *very* private person."

"Then how did you get to know him?"

I groaned inwardly. This was going to unleash a torrent of memories, many of them intensely emotional for me. I bit my lip, took a deep breath, and began, "I met him a few months after I turned nine. My mother had just died, and I was in such shaky shape that my father wasn't about to leave me at home alone when he came out to see your uncle on business."

"Jared lost his mother three years ago," Micah said quietly. "So the two of you have something in common."

"Oh, I'm so sorry," I said turning to the boy. "Now I've gone and stuck my foot in it!"

"Not at all," Micah replied with a gentle smile. "There was no way for you to know." There was something about the man that I found appealing. He had a thoughtful way about him. His calm, deep brown eyes drew you in, glowing with warmth and empathy but with a trace of sadness— maybe even loneliness—in them.

The boy also looked at me with compassion in his eyes. "It's okay," he said. "Anyway, you lost your mother, too."

"Yeah, we both know how awful that is. But your uncle helped me get through it."

"How?" The man's and boy's eyes were on me.

"Well, after Mama died, I was really sad and mixed up. I was sort of drifting along, not eating or sleeping much. Pop was so full of grief and so busy keeping the farm going that he didn't have much time or energy to take care of me. I was struggling along, doing poorly. Then one day, when Pop had to consult your uncle about a problem with our tractor, I met him. I was definitely *not* looking forward to meeting your uncle."

"Why not?"

"He had kind of a scary reputation around town. People called him 'Old Man Morrison,' because of his odd appearance and because he lived all alone out here so far away from town. Kids at school called him 'The Boogeyman'."

"Was he?"

"No, of course not. But when I knew I was going to have to meet him, I was really nervous. I didn't know what to expect."

"You said he looked odd?" Micah broke in.

"His clothes were worn thin and faded and patched to within an inch of their life. He also had deep scars on his cheek and hand, along with a noticeable limp. When I first saw him, I thought he looked like a pirate!"

"You must have been scared!"

"I was until I actually met him. As it turned out, he was so kind and gentle that, right away, I felt at ease. The first day we met, he gave me a pad and pencil and got me to start drawing. I eventually ended up going to art school in New York, and it all began with his support and encouragement."

"There's a lovely charcoal portrait of him hanging in his bedroom," Micah said. "It's the only likeness of him I've ever seen."

"Yeah, I did that portrait a few years ago." I looked closely at the man. "You mean you never knew him at all?"

"No. That's why we'd really be grateful if you would tell us everything you know about him."

"Well, there's plenty to tell, but I can't right now. I've got to head home."

The following Saturday afternoon I returned to the Morrison farm and helped the father and son harvest vegetables from their uncle's large garden. "He believed in growing as much of his own food as possible," I told them. "Next weekend, we could carve some Jack-o-lanterns for Halloween, if you want to," I suggested to Jared's delight.

The next week passed slowly for me, and I found myself eagerly looking forward to the return of the man and his boy. When Saturday finally arrived, my two youngest stepbrothers went out to Mr. M's farm with me, not wanting to miss the fun. As Micah and I stood side-by-side watching the three boys earnestly carving scary faces in their pumpkins, he quietly put his hand on my shoulder. When I went to bed that night, I could still feel it.

What did it mean? What did I want it to mean?

The next time I saw them, it was mid-November. Micah told me he'd been sorting through Mr. M's clothes and had been surprised by their unusual sizes. "Yes," I said. "He was very tall and thin—six two or three and not much over a hundred and fifty pounds. He had a lot of trouble finding clothes to fit him. Pants were near-to-impossible to find, and he always had to belt them tightly. In cold weather, he'd wear long thermal underwear. The tops would stick out of the cuffs of his shirts and the bottoms out of his Levi's when he sat down. But nothing could disguise his scrawny physique. He was strong, but he was also the thinnest man I've ever known. Pop called him 'Slim.'"

"Didn't he eat?" Jared asked.

"Actually, he ate a lot. I've seen him put away three bowls of stew or pinto beans at a single sitting, along with piles of biscuits or huge chunks of cornbread. One afternoon, he and I ate a whole pie, sort of as a snack. I'd made one out of apricots, his favorite, and we just kept talking and eating until it was all gone." Jared smiled.

The boy and his father seemed to relish my Mr. M stories, so I went on to tell them how the Morrison farm had eventually become like a second home to me.

"A pad and pencil were always waiting for me on the table in the living room. When my work started to become more advanced, your uncle supplied artist's crayons, a pen and bottle of ink, and watercolors. After a while, he even sectioned off a corner in his furniture-repair shop for me, calling it my studio. His home became my safe haven and the place where I began developing as an artist."

From the memories I found myself sharing with them, some sort of bond seemed to be forming between us— between a young woman grieving the loss of her loved ones and a lonely man and his motherless son.

Soon Thanksgiving Day was approaching. It would be my first major holiday without my father. And besides Pop, there'd be an additional reminder of loss, because Mr. M had always joined us for holiday gatherings. How would we celebrate Thanksgiving without having it ruined by sadness?

Micah and Jared planned to drive down from St. Louis on Friday after spending Thanksgiving Day there with relatives. They'd be at the Morrison farm for the rest of the long holiday weekend. As Doris and I prepared the holiday feast, I kept thinking about them and was surprised to realize how eager I was to see them again and enjoy an extra-long weekend together. Then all of a sudden I became uncomfortable. Did I really want to become overly involved with this widower and his boy? Wasn't my goal in life to become an established artist? What would happen to my painting if I were to become a wife and mother? Women were now talking about "having it all"—both a family *and* a career. But I was only a year out of art school, with no real "career" in sight. Wouldn't it be wise to nip this blossoming friendship in the bud?

And yet I couldn't seem to get the man and his son out of my mind . . . .

Thanksgiving Day came and went, and the next day dawned. Micah and Jared planned to stop at our farmhouse to pick me up on their way back to the Morrison place. In spite of my reservations and concerns, my heart leapt with excitement when I saw their car pull into our farmhouse driveway. As Doris later told me, "It was as if a light bulb lit up inside you. You came alive."

We spent the day gathering wood for the Morrison farmhouse's stoves and fireplaces. I showed Jared and his father how Mr. M had taught me to cut and split logs. In the barn, I retrieved the old cross-cut saw that Mr. M called "Old Gappy." "Your uncle and Pop and I cut down many a tree with 'Old Gappy,'" I told them.

"How does it work?" Jared asked.

We found a downed tree of medium size in a near corner of the property. I positioned the saw against the bark of the tree and ran it lightly back and forth until the teeth were set into the wood, ready for cutting. "Now you take the other end," I told the boy. "The main thing to remember is to let the saw do the work. We just need to guide the blade back and forth across the trunk, taking turns pulling it toward us until the log's been cut through."

As we worked, I could feel Micah's eyes on me—warm, kind eyes that seemed to be smiling with pleasure and gratitude.

Before long, we had several good-sized logs ready to be split. Though I hadn't used a splitting maul for a while, I hadn't forgotten how. "Keep your eyes on where you want the blade to fall, and it will hit the log dead center," I said, repeating the advice their uncle had passed along to me. After a few tries, my log popped open with a satisfying crack. Jared wouldn't have the height or heft to swing the maul efficiently until he got more growth on him. But when I showed him how to hammer an iron wedge into the center seam of the log, he did a fine job of splitting it cleanly.

"What's happening to me?" I asked myself that night as I lay in bed. "I'm sharing some of my most personal memories with this guy and his kid. I'd better watch out or my plans to become a professional artist could end up going down the drain."

Or would they? Since Pop's death, I had been helping Doris and my oldest stepbrother manage the farm. It was hard at first, but Pop fortunately had a competent crew of farm hands—experienced workers hired from the local group home who knew their way around the farm, guided by supervisors who oversaw their work. Soon, with minimal instructions from Doris or me, they were able to keep the farm running fairly efficiently, providing me with time to return to my painting.

As a result, I found myself settling into a pattern: working on my drawings and paintings on the weekdays and spending the weekend days with the man and his boy. It was a pattern I enjoyed immensely, but in the back of my mind I still worried about keeping a balance between our deepening friendship and my goal of being a serious artist.

And yet, at the same time, it was also becoming increasingly important to me—for my own sake—that Micah and Jared should know and love Mr. M as much as I had. Although it was painful to recall the details of their uncle's life—and, by association, Pop's—I discovered that sharing my memories felt like honoring the two men who'd most influenced my life, helping me to push through my grief in the process. I also couldn't ignore the fact that something had stirred inside me when I first saw Jared, who was about the same age as I'd been when I'd lost Mama. Though I'd never really thought I had a maternal bone in my body, I found that I now wanted to protect and nurture the boy and make everything all right for him and his father. I'd sensed something in both of them—a hunger and loneliness, a yearning for love and companionship. From our first meeting Mr. M and I had sensed these same longings in each other—

longings that now seemed to be coming full circle with his great-nephew and great-great nephew and me.

And then there were my growing feelings for Jared's father. . . .

November turned into December. Soon it would be Christmas—another major holiday without Pop and Mr. M. Again, Doris and I were determined to try to make things as festive as possible. It helped that, other than spending Christmas Eve and Christmas Day with their St. Louis relatives, Micah and Jared had decided to spend the bulk of Jared's winter break from school at the Morrison farm. They would consequently be frequent visitors to the Everheart farm, where the twins had decided to take the boy under their wing as an honorary little brother.

The first order of business was to bake cookies. Lots of cookies—for us, and with plenty left over to give as presents to our friends and neighbors and local shut-ins. Jared joined in enthusiastically, cutting out and decorating pan after pan of trees and bells and Santas before tackling the gingerbread men. Doris made the more elaborate rum balls and pressed butter cookies. And at the twins' insistence, we made the Rice Krispies balls I'd invented for them the first Christmas after they'd become part of our family, the regular Rice Krispies-marshmallow mixture shaped into balls and rolled in sprinkles. "Christmas wouldn't be Christmas without them!" the twins always said.

And winter break wouldn't have been winter break without snow. Fortunately, we were blessed with plenty of it for the boys to frolic in. We tramped all over both of the farms, building snowmen and sledding. Jared was almost beside himself with joy when Doris and the twins presented him with his own sled for Christmas.

All too soon, it was the next-to-last day of the father and son's winter vacation in Plainfield. Micah had to spend the day at Mr. M's place working on a manuscript that was due upon his return to his job as an editor at Normandy

Publications in St. Louis. While he worked, Jared and I peeled and cut half a bushel of apples to make applesauce for them to take home with them. We had a pot of it simmering by the time Micah joined us for a classic cold-weather lunch of tomato soup and grilled cheese sandwiches.

After lunch, when Micah returned to his editing, Jared and I set out to explore Mr. M's orchards and beyond. The day had turned bitterly cold, so we dressed in our warmest clothes and donned tall boots to slog through the snow drifts. I tucked a thermos of hot chocolate and a packet of Christmas cookies into a knapsack along with my sketchbook.

The orchard was stark—almost haunting—with the bare limbs of the trees looking like rows of splayed out gray-brown bones. The boughs of the cedars hugging the boundaries of the property hung heavy with snow. It was quiet and still. I executed a couple of quick sketches and made a mental note to return before the snow melted in order to more fully capture the pristine splendor.

"Let's walk down to the pond to see how that renegade apple tree's doing," I suggested. Jared knew the one I was talking about: a stray that decades earlier had toppled into the pond so that the trunk remained half-rooted on the bank with the top semi-submerged in the water. It'd been an intriguing subject for several drawings I planned to turn into tempera paintings.

"Okay," the boy said, but his voice betrayed a lack of his usual enthusiasm.

We trudged along without talking. The only sounds that broke the silence were the crunch of our footsteps and the huffing of our breath propelling little white puffs of fog into the air.

Jared looked melancholy. "You all right?" I asked him.

"Yeah."

His reply sounded shaky. And, in fact, *he* was shaky. My hand shot out to steady him when he stumbled into a snow bank.

Almost immediately, his arms were around me, hugging me as if he never intended to let go. "I don't want to go back! I don't want to go back!" he cried. "I might never see you again!"

I didn't know what to say, so I continued to hold him until he was ready to release me. He grasped my hand and held on tight.

We continued making our way to the pond. The banks were snow-covered and the water as frozen as a skating rink. It was a lovely scene but a bleak one that matched Jared's mood. There before us was the apple tree, resting without a care in the world, with its trunk half in and half out of the water. It seemed as good a spot as any for us to stop. In no time flat, we cleared two stumps and sat down.

"Hot chocolate?" I asked the boy.

"Maybe a little," he mumbled.

I poured a half a thermos cupful and handed it to him. "Cookies?"

"Maybe later."

I let Jared take a few sips of his hot drink. When the time seemed right, I said, "It's sort of scary, isn't it?" The boy looked at me big-eyed. "What I mean is, anytime we have to say goodbye to somebody we like a lot—even if it's only for a short time—it can be kind of frightening."

I thought I saw Jared nod, so I kept talking. "It's probably extra hard for you and me because we lost our mamas."

Jared's breath caught in a half-sob, but I pressed on. "I mean, all of a sudden, they were just *gone*."

Jared looked as woebegone as a boy could be.

"And now, in just a couple of days, you and your father will be in St. Louis while I'm still back here in Plainfield. And it may be weeks before you're down here again. Of course, we'll see each other again. And we'll talk a lot on the phone." I reached out and squeezed Jared's hand. "But we *will* see each other again. We *will* be together again."

"How d'you know?" His voice was rough, insistent. "Can you guarantee it?"

"Well nobody can be 100 percent sure. But I'd say we can be 99 percent sure, and that's about as close as you can get to a total guarantee."

In an effort to diffuse the intensity of the conversation, I poured some hot chocolate into the extra cup I'd packed and took a sip. "Mmmmmm! This hits the spot!"

The boy's lips twitched with the tiniest of half smiles.

I dived back into the conversation. "You do know how much I care for you and your father."

"I want to be on this farm with you," Jared blurted out. "I want us all to be together!"

"I'd like that, too," I said. And despite my passion to be an artist, I meant it. Oh, the things I wanted to do for that man and his son!

"But what if you died?" the boy's voice trembled.

"Well, I don't plan to anytime soon," I replied. "Neither did Pop," a nasty little voice inside my head shot back at me. I quickly suppressed a shudder.

"But what if?"

I put down my cup and looked at him. "You mean like your mother?"

Well, there it was.

Though I'd figured the two of us would have a conversation about this some day, I hadn't planned on having it so soon—and certainly not while sitting on tree stumps in frigid snow.

"I suppose anytime we have to say goodbye—even for a little while—there's always that fear of 'what if?'"

Jared shivered but otherwise seemed to be holding steady. He inched his stump closer to mine until they were almost touching.

"It's a risk, isn't it, to become really attached to someone—to sort of give our heart to someone?"

"I really like *you!*" Jared cried out. "I've given *you* my heart. I love you . . . and I know Dad does, too!"

I felt flushed, dizzy, disoriented. My God! How had things gotten this far? Had I led them on in any way? I knew I'd better be careful. "Yes, it's also risky for your father," I finally got out, "but in a different way from you."

Jared stared at his mitten-clad hands, grave and quiet but not closed into himself, so I said, "Tell me what you remember about your mother."

He didn't say anything, so I started the conversation by saying, "I remember how my mama used to read to me. She always did the *best* voices when she acted out all the characters in the stories and poems. She used different voices for each one and really made their personalities come alive!"

Jared turned to me, his expression suddenly animated. "My mom did that too!" he said. "I remember her voice . . . and her laugh, when something crazy happened, like in *How the Grinch Stole Christmas*. She did the *best* Grinch voice. She loved that story and the cartoon movie, too. We'd watch it a couple of times a day in the week before Christmas. And she'd use that Grinch voice other times, too, just to make me laugh."

My heart went out to the boy. "Oh, and remember how they'd hold us and hug us? I'd be so close to Mama that her blouses and sweaters were pressed into my cheek and I'd breathe in the scent of her soap and shampoo. It was like the two of us were in our own private, secret little world."

Jared smiled. "Mom used to give me graham crackers with milk and peanut butter and jelly sandwiches. When I had alphabet soup with crackers, we'd pick out the letters and spell our names. She would sit with me while I ate, and we'd make up stories and laugh and talk."

"You know, nothing can ever take those memories away from us," I said quietly. "And nothing can take away all the memories we've had here together in Plainfield. We'll treasure them forever. And I know we'll have a whole lot more." My brain was telling me: "Back off—don't get drawn in too deep." My heart was telling me to fold the boy in my arms and tell him I loved him.

Before the conversation could turn somber again, I poured us some more hot chocolate, then reached into my knapsack and pulled out the packet of cookies. When we bit into them, the multi-colored sprinkles we'd decorated them with exploded all over the pristine white snow around us, making us laugh. It was then I noticed how very cold it had become. "My God! It's *freezing* out here! My rear end has turned into a block of ice!" With that, we headed back to the Morrison farmhouse, arriving to the aroma of simmering applesauce and the warmth of a fire snapping in the Franklin stove in the living room.

That night, Micah and I slept together. It began innocently. Shortly after Jared and I returned to the farmhouse, it began snowing heavily. Soon, we were engulfed in a blizzard that made driving hazardous. "Maybe you should stay here," Micah said. "Have supper with us and spend the night here." I telephoned Doris and let her know my change of plans.

As the three of us sat together in the warm, cozy kitchen with an Ozark blizzard howling outside, I suddenly felt more at home than I'd ever felt in my life, nurturing and nurtured with my own little family around me. As my brain and heart continued to struggle about what I should do, it was becoming clearer and clearer that my brain was fighting a losing battle.

After supper, we wandered into the living room, where Micah opened the door of the Franklin stove and we toasted marshmallows. When Jared went to bed, Micah and I continued to sit before the fire, silently staring at the flames. After a while, he put his arm around me, and I snuggled against him. We began kissing. One thing led to another . . . .

We made love gently and tenderly and passionately. Nothing rushed. Nothing forced. It was as natural and fundamental as breathing. "So this is what it's supposed to be like!" something inside me exalted as I held his body tightly.

We didn't get much sleep that night. At some point, the snowplow came through. The next morning when Jared came into the kitchen, Micah and I were sipping coffee and trying our best to appear as calm and collected as possible after our night of uninhibited intimacy, but I could feel myself glowing all over.

And then it was time for me to go. Micah and Jared shoveled a path to Pop's pickup. I hugged them and was on my way—but not before Micah and I had made plans to talk on the phone every night before bedtime.

As the new year began, my mind was full of unresolved questions. Where was I going with my life? Was I going to be an artist or a wife and mother? Where was all this leading?

To give myself some structure during the long winter months while Micah and Jared were back in St. Louis, I decided to begin an ambitious series of Andrew Wyeth-style portrait paintings—stark character sketches of anonymous Ozark men and women who in one way or another represented the culture of the region. Each individual portrait would try to convey something basic about Ozark people—some essential characteristic of the region's inhabitants as they struggled to survive in their hardscrabble economy:

- An elderly farmer in bib overalls and a John Deere cap, with an expression of stoic perseverance on his weather-beaten face reflecting a half-century of battling the forces of nature to produce the corn and hogs that his family's survival depended on.

- A worn-down farmwife with a toddler clinging to her leg, her pinched, wind-wrinkled face reflecting a life of unrelenting childcare, wood-hauling, and food preparation.

- A bearded hunter in a camouflage jacket cradling a deer rifle in his arms and exuding an aura of fierce self-sufficiency in his cold, steely eyes.

- A heavily mascaraed diner waitress leaning wearily against a kitchen wall during her coffee break, stoop-shouldered from years of work and abuse but with a survivor's glint of defiant toughness in her eyes.

- A grease-stained mechanic intently examining an engine part with the calm self-confidence of the uneducated jack-of-all-trades who knows intuitively how to keep any sort of machine running.

- A hippie couple in bandannas and tie-dyed T-shirts holding a tray of marijuana plants and smiling in back-to-the-land contentment.

The portrait series was the kind of big, challenging project that would push me to elevate my technical skills as an artist. I would need to paint peoples' facial expressions—the look in their eye, the tilt of their eyebrow, the set of their mouth, the texture of their skin—with a subtlety and a sophistication that I hadn't previously attempted. If I succeeded in pulling it off, I thought I might capture part of the cultural essence, part of the collective soul, of the place where I grew up.

I threw myself into the project. Before I knew it, March had come, and with it the promise of spring and new beginnings. But most important of all, with the weather easing, Micah and Jared would now be returning more regularly to the Morrison farm. We had talked almost every night over the phone, but it wasn't the same as being with them.

During their first weekend visit at the end of the month, Micah announced that he and Jared had decided to spend the upcoming summer on the farm. Jared missed the farm, and spending time with me and my family, so much so that he'd begged his father to let them stay in Plainfield for all three months. Micah shared his sentiments. In fact, he'd already begun to arrange with his employer to do his editing from the farm, with occasional overnight trips back to St. Louis to pick up and deliver manuscripts.

A large part of me thrilled at this news, but I also felt apprehensive. Now there would be no way for me to sidestep the "career-versus-relationship" issue I was still struggling with.

In early June, Micah and Jared moved to the farm full-time. Jared had received a bicycle for his birthday and spent hours wheeling all over the property. He'd also decided to build a fort. He poked around the farm and found plenty of old wood for this project in the rafters of the barn and in the cider house. One of the crew members gave him some pointers to help get him started, but the boy was determined to design and build the fort by himself, complete with a sleeping bunk, door, and window—an enterprise that would occupy him for a good part of the summer.

I showed Micah some of my Ozark portraits-in-progress, and he was lavish with his praise, telling me he thought they were "evocative" and "moving." One afternoon, out of the blue, he asked: "What if we fixed up my uncle's old woodworking shop as an office for me and a studio for you? I'll take the bottom floor, and you can have the top floor, which has wonderful light. Then you can work from here."

"So," I thought, "he understands how important my painting is to me." I'd occasionally tried to warn him that I wasn't a typical woman, and it didn't appear to faze him. Instead, he seemed to want to encourage my work and arrange things so that I could have a serious relationship with him without derailing my progress as an artist.

By midsummer, the three of us were closer than ever, and although I still had misgivings about where this was heading, my concerns were fading fast.

Meanwhile, Jared was thriving on the farm and didn't want to leave, even to accompany his father on trips back to St. Louis. His heart's desire was to live full-time on the Morrison farm. It didn't take long for him to begin lobbying for his father to let him switch schools. Micah didn't need much convincing. He, too, was in his element—relaxed and contented and comfortable editing at home in his Levi's and work boots.

On one of his trips back to St. Louis, Micah met with his bosses to discuss the possibility of his working year-round from the farm. Over the summer, he'd demonstrated that the volume of his editing hadn't suffered by working remotely from Plainfield, and, in fact, he'd been able take on even more manuscripts. To help facilitate this plan, I stayed with Jared or brought him with me to the Everheart farm to be spoiled by Doris and my stepbrothers whenever his father had to return to St. Louis.

Soon Micah had arranged for Jared to enroll in Plainfield Elementary. That September, the boy began fourth grade at his new school and settled into Ozark life as if he was born to it.

Then one sultry afternoon, Micah stormed into my studio. "Jared loves you and needs you, and so do I," he announced. "It's time we got married and became a family."

Without even pausing to think, I said, "I love you and I need you, too, Micah, but I don't want to disappoint the two of you. I'm afraid I can never be the 'normal' little homemaker you'd both need me to be. I've come too far in my painting to give it up now."

"Who wants 'normal'?" Micah shot back. "In case you haven't noticed, Jared and I are pretty self-sufficient. We love you just the way you are. We know how important it is for you to be able to continue to paint. Why do you think I wanted you to have a studio here on the farm?"

My brain was reeling, but my heart had already made my decision for me. "I always thought I'd have to choose between having a family or a career," I murmured, as much to myself as to him.

"Who says you can't have both?"

Micah and I were married that October. His father deeded the farm over to us as a wedding present. "Eventually, it will come to Micah anyway," he said. "And now's the time you need a place of your own the most."

It had been an emotionally turbulent period in my life— the most turbulent I had ever known. In the space of fifteen months, I had lost my father and my two closest friends, and found a husband and a stepson. Plainfield's preachers would undoubtedly have had a tidy explanation for it all— something like: "When God closes a door, He opens a window," or some such. As far as I could tell, however, it was just the rollercoaster of life continuing to buffet me along unpredictably in directions I hadn't seen coming. All I knew was that a new phase of my life was beginning. And it felt right.

Having It All

SIX MONTHS INTO MY MARRIAGE with Micah Morrison, I was finding life as a wife and mother to be more complicated than I'd imagined. Though my husband and stepson, Jared, understood—and made allowances for—the demands of my artistic life, I now had many other responsibilities as well. There were meals to prepare—gone were my days of nibbling on cheese and crackers or eating a sandwich on the run—along with grocery shopping, house cleaning, a husband to keep contented, and a child to nurture and keep clothed and clean. It was difficult, sometimes, to find enough uninterrupted time to work on the painting that was the focus of my creative aspirations.

Part of this situation was my own fault. I was still feeling my way into my new life as a wife and mother, and although determined—driven—to draw and paint, I wasn't about to short-change Micah or Jared or fail to look after their needs.

Despite my new responsibilities, I kept pushing ahead with the Ozark portrait series that I'd begun the previous winter. I now expanded the scope of the project, adding new character studies—many of which seemed to subconsciously reflect my inner feelings about my new role in life.

Every once in a while, when I could find the time, I'd get into Old Reliable, my late friend Mr. M's beat-up pickup, and drive the unpaved back roads looking for glimpses of backwoods inhabitants and their dwellings, doing quick sketches or snapping Polaroid photos of potential subjects for paintings. I increasingly found myself attracted to images of work-worn farmwomen, women I now could identify with more closely. Though the particulars of our lives were different, I suddenly began to feel that I *knew* them—knew in my bones, sinews, and muscles how constrained and overburdened they must feel.

In one variation, I sketched a farmwife bent over a rake—was she using it as a garden tool or as a prop to hold up her weary body?—removing leaves from the beds of newly emerging asparagus shoots. In another sketch, a middle-aged woman—her face smudged with sweat and soil—knelt prayer-like, planting seedlings in neatly hoed rows in her truck garden with a toddler at her heels digging in the dirt. Another study portrayed a rawboned mother and her daughter sitting on a farmhouse porch, plucking feathers from a pair of newly slaughtered chickens—a pail of steaming innards at their feet.

Besides feeling a kinship with the farmwomen, I could also identify—thanks to all the years I'd helped my father on our farm—with the lives of the farmers I observed during my drives in the countryside. I quick-sketched a grizzled old-timer struggling with leather-gloved hands to tighten a sagging barbed wire fence along the edge of his field. A burly middle-aged man building a stone wall also captured my interest as I watched him meticulously stack rocks of all shapes and sizes heaved up from the never-ending supply in his fields.

I continued to devote as much time as possible to my artistic work, but I increasingly began to worry that I was becoming too distracted by my household duties, too fragmented, too worn out, to ever become an actual professional artist.

During Christmas of our first full year together, I broke down in a crisis of self-doubt—probably brought on, at least in part, by the seemingly non-stop cookie-baking, gift-wrapping, home-decorating, and countless other preparations that regularly drive women to their knees during the holidays.

On Christmas Eve, Micah walked into our farmhouse kitchen and found me crying at the sink while doing the dishes. "What's the matter?" he asked in a concerned voice.

"I'm not sure who I am anymore, or what I even want to be," I blurted out between sobs. "I'm trying to work on my painting, but all it's doing is taking me away from the time I need to look after you and Jared. What's the point? It's not like I'm ever going to become some famous artist or anything. Maybe I'm just kidding myself. It all seems so pointless—so self-indulgent . . . so selfish."

"Well, first of all," Micah said, taking me in his arms, "you're trying to do too much, and it's draining you. Why not let Jared and me take over some of the household jobs for you? You can show him how to run a few loads of laundry through the washer and dryer every week as part of his Sunday chores. And I can do the cooking three or four nights a week. I cooked the meals every day for four years as a single parent, so it's not like I don't know how to do it. My specialties are hot dogs and Campbell's soup, canned spaghetti with meatballs, and—for special occasions—fish sticks and tater tots. It may not be gourmet cuisine, but, hell, at least we won't starve to death. And it'll buy you more time to work on your portraits. They're too good—and you've worked too hard on them—for you to give them up now."

He went on to say that he also thought it was time for me to start exhibiting my painting in public and see what kind of response it received. "How are you ever going to know how good you are if you don't put your work out there?"

"Well, maybe you're right," I said, drying my eyes. "Back in high school I entered my stuff in a couple of statewide contests for student artists. Maybe there are some venues like that for adult artists."

Over the next several weeks, I glanced through various midwestern art journals and newsletters to see if I could find any opportunities to show my work.

As it turned out, I didn't have to look far. One Sunday morning, Micah handed me the weekend edition of the *Springfield News-Leader,* where I read about a call for artists to submit their work for a local juried art show to be held in the same Springfield Armory where I'd shown my work as a teenager. But this time the stakes were higher—any work in the show judged to be of special merit would be entered in a group exhibition to be held the following month in the Wentworth Gallery in downtown Springfield. Everything displayed in the gallery exhibition would be available for sale.

For the Armory show, each artist was allowed to submit up to four works of art. I decided to enter the strongest and most polished versions of my first Ozark portraits in tempera: a weather-beaten old farmer; an exhausted farmwife with a baby clinging to her leg; a cold-eyed hunter cradling his rifle; and a grease-stained mechanic tinkering with an engine part.

To my astonishment—and my immense gratification—all four of my submissions were selected for inclusion in the show. And to my even greater astonishment and gratification, all four of them received "meritorious" ratings from the judges, who found them to be "starkly realistic and subtly haunting" representations of Ozark life.

A month later, Micah, Jared, and I attended my "opening" in the Wentworth Gallery's group exhibit.

It was a formal affair—a gala event unlike anything I'd attended since my New York City days. The art was beautifully displayed on off-white walls, accompanied by biographical information about each artist. Since the exhibition had been well-publicized, the gallery's rooms were full. The reception was understated but elegant, featuring a variety of fine wines, cheeses, fruit, and canapés. Everyone in the Springfield art community attended—or at least put in an appearance—with the artists standing beside their creations, answering questions and discussing their influences and techniques. A range of genres from realism to minimalism to expressionism to pop art was represented, each with its aficionados. I overheard someone mention that my paintings looked "Wyethian," and although I would never have presumed to make such a claim, the comparison pleased me enormously.

The portraits of the farmer and farmwife sold within days, followed a couple of weeks later by the hunter and the mechanic. The Gallery's owners had priced them at $500 each, with the artist receiving 50 percent of the selling price. Suddenly, unbelievably, I was making money from my art— not Big Money, but money all the same.

Among the people who attended the Wentworth Gallery exhibition were two junior faculty members from the graduate program in art at Washington University in St. Louis. Shortly after the exhibition closed, they contacted me with an invitation to participate in an exhibition of "Up-and-Coming Young Regional Artists" that they were organizing at Washington University's Kemper Art Museum. Starting from total obscurity, I was apparently now emerging as an "up-and-coming young regional artist." What a hoot!

At the end of the Kemper show, the museum's acquisitions committee purchased one of my submissions—a tempera study of two young hippies with a tray of marijuana seedlings—for the museum's permanent collection. Suddenly, the up-and-coming young regional artist was beginning to acquire some serious credentials . . . and a bit of a reputation, too.

Back in my home studio in Plainfield, I pushed ahead with my Ozark portraiture with a new seriousness, working around my housework and shopping as time permitted.

As I did so, I began to notice that Jared, having witnessed his stepmother's recent artistic triumphs first-hand, was starting to pay more attention to my work in the studio, watching my techniques and processes with a new interest.

Over the next several weeks, I often caught him looking over my shoulder, quietly observing what was taking shape on my sketchpad or canvas. I also noticed him examining my pencils and brushes, my charcoals and watercolors, my paints and inks and crayons. I sensed that he was becoming increasingly interested in trying to do what I was doing.

One day I handed him a pad and pencil. "Draw what you see," I said, repeating what Mr. M, my first mentor, had told me so many years earlier. Sure enough, the boy not only had an interest in drawing but a real aptitude for it . . . and an eagerness to improve.

I began to oversee Jared's progress, responding to his questions and encouraging him to draw every day.

He flourished in the studio. Before long, I made a special place for him to work. Every now and then, I'd offer a suggestion or demonstrate a technique. I didn't have to say anything twice—the kid was a natural. His sketches of our farm's outbuildings and cider house were better than anything I could have done at his age.

Gradually, as his drawing skills became more and more developed, his teachers at Plainfield Middle School began to take notice. Some of his classmates also—out of admiration or jealously or both—became increasingly interested in his drawings, and a few parents made inquiries at the school about how they could nurture their children's newfound interest in art. Though the art classes taught in the school were adequate for most students, they weren't personalized or advanced enough for children with genuine creative potential.

After learning that Jared was receiving personal instruction at home from me, it didn't take long for the mothers of some of Jared's classmates to approach me, asking—almost beseeching—me to provide their children with extracurricular instruction.

Oh dear! As if being a wife, a mother, and a working artist wasn't challenging enough, how was I supposed to take on additional responsibilities as a part-time art instructor as well? On the other hand, how in good conscience could I say no? Besides, what better way to give back to my community?

And above all, what better way to honor the memory of the two people—both now sadly deceased—who had done so much to help me get started: my benefactor Mr. M, who had first introduced me to the rewards of making art, and my high school art teacher Ms. MacLerren, who had encouraged me to pursue my painting seriously?

In the end, against my better judgment, I agreed to take on six students for a Saturday morning class in my studio on our farm. Soon, however, word got out and I began receiving additional requests for instruction. Within two months, the space in my small studio had become inadequate to our needs.

As the requests for instruction continued to come in and the number of students grew to nearly fifteen, it became increasingly obvious that I needed to find a larger facility. It had also become clear that it would be better to hold classes closer to the center of Plainfield, in a location more convenient for the students and their parents than our out-of-the-way farm.

"What you really ought to do," one of the parents suggested one Saturday, "is set up a small art school in town."

Micah and I talked about the idea, and he thought it might be doable, with enough money and energy . . . and, of course, the right location. And best of all, he pointed out, if I managed to get an instructional studio up and running in town, I might eventually be able to recruit a part-time instructor or two, so I could get back to devoting more time to my own work.

We soon began looking around town for a suitable place. A few weeks later, a former Baptist church three blocks from

Plainfield's Main Street became available for purchase. The Baptists had recently constructed a large new church in town, and their small former church was now boarded up and on the market. From the outside, the building looked a bit like the classic country church pictured in Grant Wood's painting "American Gothic." It was being sold by our local realtor, Oldest Hills Properties, for a daunting asking price of $39,000.

The church building would need some interior remodeling, but it was in good shape, and its large floor-to-ceiling windows made it ideal for use as an art studio.

But even if we could find the resources to buy the place, there were additional complications. The realtors informed us that before we got any further into discussions about the property, I would need the permission of the county's Baptist church deaconship to buy it.

Accordingly, I quickly contacted the Plainfield Baptist deacon's office and asked if I could attend their next board meeting to present my case for buying the church. At that meeting, before a board consisting of three very serious and rather dour-looking deacons, I emphasized the need for the kind of art school I was proposing and spelled out how in a multitude of ways it would not only benefit the community but also reflect well on their organization in making their building available for such a noble purpose.

The deacons were not particularly receptive to my proposal because it meant that the building would be used for secular purposes, whereas they had been hoping that the congregation of some smaller local church would buy it.

"Good grief!" I thought to myself. "Do we really need another Praise Jesus Pentecostal church in Plainfield rather than a safe and secure place for a few of the kids in town to develop some artistic skills?"

"You know, gentlemen," I said. "This art school could be considered part of your Christian ministry's secular outreach program."

One of the deacons seemed inclined to be flexible, but a second deacon—a man named Martin Elliot—was outspoken in his objection to my proposal, declaring that he was dead set against it because we were planning to use the property's building and grounds for a blatantly non-religious venture.

Elliot was a heavy-set, ruddy-faced man with a crew-cut, dressed in a too-tight-fitting JCPenney's dress shirt and tie, with a plastic pencil-sleeve in his shirt pocket. "Remember your First Corinthians, little missy," he told me condescendingly, "where Paul tells us that 'he who defiles the Lord's temple will suffer eternal damnation.'"

Eternal damnation? I was tempted to ask him how that fit in with Matthew's account of Jesus saying "suffer the little children to come to me and do not hinder them, for the Kingdom of Heaven belongs to such as these"—which was exactly what I was trying to do with the art school—but I thought I'd better hold my tongue and not antagonize him any further.

Deacon Elliot continued, arguing forcefully that, with patience, he *knew* their former church building would find a suitable buyer in the form of one of the small country churches in the area that was looking to relocate into town and expand its work spreading "The Word." Although he didn't actually come out and say it, I sensed that part of his opposition stemmed from the fact that I was a woman.

The third deacon—potentially the deciding vote—was Elliot's son-in-law and would undoubtedly follow his relative's lead.

Along with Deacon Elliot's opposition, money was a major obstacle. We estimated that in addition to the $39,000 asking price, it would take at least another $5,000 to remodel the facility for instructional purposes and equipment. All of a sudden, the art-school idea was beginning to seem more and more like a pipe dream.

I was still stewing over the project's seemingly intractable obstacles several days after the board meeting when out of the blue I received a telephone call from Clarissa Billington.

Mrs. Billington was a well-known figure in town. She was generally thought of as Plainfield's dowager empress—its behind-the-scenes mover and shaker. Though many townspeople had never seen her, nearly everyone knew about her. She was the widow of Walter Billington, the former president of the First National Bank of Plainfield. Twenty-five years earlier, while returning from an annual state bank executives' conference, she and her husband had been involved in a serious automobile accident that had killed her husband and left her crippled from the waist down and permanently confined to a wheelchair.

Her husband's estate had made her the wealthiest woman in town. And, although she wasn't often seen in public, she was widely known for her local philanthropic activities—as, for example, when she had funded a new children's reading room for the public library entirely out of her own pocket.

Unbeknownst to me, Mrs. Billington—who was now in her mid-seventies—was the grandmother of one of Jared's classmates, a girl who was attending my Saturday morning classes. From her, Mrs. Billington had heard about the possibility of my establishing an art school in Plainfield, and she had felt compelled to call me. Mrs. Billington explained that she would like to hear more about my idea and asked if I would stop by her home and tell her more.

In a nervous-sounding voice, I told her I would be happy to.

The following day, I found myself standing at the colonnaded front door of a palatial house in a section of Plainfield that members of the Everheart family seldom visited. "You're moving up in the world, Hallie Jo Everheart," I told myself. "Let's hope you're not in over your head."

A man in a dark suit opened the door and ushered me into the foyer, from where I could see a small figure in a wheelchair seated at a large desk in an office off the elegantly decorated living room.

"A Ms. Everheart to see you," the man announced. Mrs. Billington looked up and gestured for me to enter. Taking a deep breath, I walked in.

Mrs. Billington was a small, slender woman, no taller than my five feet four inches. Her hair, styled in a short, easy bob, fell in a flattering profusion of soft silver waves around her face, partially concealing several deep scars on her forehead. She wore no makeup except for a smudge of eye shadow and a light coating of neutral lipstick and was dressed in tailored black slacks paired with an expensive looking rose-colored silk blouse. All in all, she radiated quiet strength, sharp intelligence, rock-solid integrity, and money.

"Please, do sit down," she said, with a trace of a gentle Ozark drawl. She asked if I'd care for tea. Immediately, a middle-aged woman appeared.

"This is Celeste," Mrs. Billington introduced her warmly. "She's my assistant . . . and so much more." Celeste exited the room and quickly returned with a tray bearing a delicately hand-painted Limoges china teapot and matching cups and saucers. Mrs. Billington poured me a cup and handed it to me.

"Thank you, Mrs. Billington," I said.

"Don't be so formal with me," she responded. "If we're going to do business together, you must call me Clarissa."

"Do business together?" I thought. "And you must call me Hallie," I replied.

She asked me to tell her about my ideas for a community art school.

As I sketched out the concept for her, it was evident that Mrs. Billington was quietly evaluating me. Looking into her eyes, I felt that she was appraising me, taking stock of an unknown local Ozark girl who apparently had some artistic talent and a desire to share that talent with promising students in the community.

When I finished laying out my plan and describing the financial obstacles I was facing, she smiled and said, "I think it's admirable. I want to help you.

"My granddaughter Amelia is taking your Saturday classes, and she's already blossoming in her drawing. I think it would be wonderful if other children who may not have the resources for extracurricular lessons could take your classes too.

"Frankly," she said, "I think your art school could make an *enormous* difference in the lives of some of the kids around here. It could help counteract the stereotype of Ozark girls as 'barefoot and pregnant at fifteen' and might keep a few of the boys from getting into serious, even criminal, mischief." She pursed her lips. "I get so *tired* of outsiders automatically disparaging Ozark culture and automatically assuming we can't accomplish anything of value."

She went on. "When I was growing up in the boondocks outside Pine Bluff, Arkansas—smart, bookish, and dirt-poor—I would have killed to have been able to attend an art school like the one you're proposing. I had some potential talent but nowhere to turn for any training. I want Amelia and her friends to have the opportunity I never had.

"So let's get down to the nuts and bolts. You've found a suitable building and you're in the process of going after it. You'll need to remodel it—take out the altar and pews, put up partitions for classrooms, and buy easels and tables and art supplies."

"Only if I can find the money to buy the place," I interjected.

"I wouldn't worry too much about that. This is *going* to happen, Hallie! I'll provide the funds to buy and renovate the building, and we can apply for grants from the Missouri Arts Council, the Chamber of Commerce, and some other likely sources in the area to cover the annual operating expenses. I'm pretty good at grant-writing, and I'm fairly well-connected. This is right up the Arts Council's alley."

Overwhelmed emotionally and with tears welling up in my eyes, I collected myself enough to warn her that there was another serious obstacle to face: the hostility of the Baptist governing board, particularly Deacon Martin Elliot, who was on record as saying that it would be a cold day in Hell before the property would be used for secular purposes.

"Well," Mrs. Billington sniffed. "We'll just see about that!" With that, she picked up the telephone and began making a call. Assuming that our meeting was over, I got up to leave.

"Stay here and listen," she told me. "This should be fun."

Turning back to her phone call, she said, "Yes, may I speak with Martin Elliot, please? . . . Marty? This is Clarissa. The reason I'm calling is to let you know that I strongly support the sale of the old church and its conversion into a local art center." Her voice, warm and pleasant up to this point, suddenly began to develop a steely edge. "I understand . . . . I understand . . . . But if you and your board want me to continue with my donations to underwrite the construction of your new church, I *strongly suggest* you sell the old building to Ms. Everheart." She let that message settle in for a few seconds and then added, "I also strongly suggest that you drop your asking price down to the property's fair market value . . . which I'd say is closer to $25,000."

There was some backwards and forwards discussion, at the end of which she said in her sweetest southern drawl: "Well, you take my suggestions back to the board and let me know what y'all decide."

Ten months later, after we secured the building and completed the necessary renovations, the Billington Art Center opened its doors. Grants and donations from the state arts council, the local chamber of commerce, and the First National Bank of Plainfield provided operating funds and supplies.

In addition, flush with excitement, I had called the parents of my late art teacher Ms. MacLerren to tell them about my new venture—one that would have thrilled their daughter no end. Mr. and Mrs. MacLerren immediately volunteered to establish a $10,000 endowment for "Madelyn MacLerren Fellowships" that would bring one or two advanced art students from Washington University in St. Louis and Southwest Missouri State in Springfield to the art school each semester to help with basic instruction and work on their own projects.

I was floored by the MacLerrens' offer. "That's an enormous amount of money for you to commit to the school!" I stammered.

They countered by saying that they'd wanted to do something like this to honor their talented daughter, who'd had so much to give before she was tragically taken from them—and from us all—so young. "She loved teaching and painting. If she were still alive, we know she would want to be a part of this. And besides," they added, "with Madelyn gone, who else are we going to leave our money to?"

Soon, thanks to the generosity of Clarissa Billington and the MacLerrens, along with the support of the Plainfield community, the new art school was developing into everything I had imagined and more—providing children's instruction at basic, intermediate, and advanced levels, and even offering a series of adult education classes for senior citizens and other town residents.

The local school system's art teachers were delighted to have extracurricular instruction available to their more promising students. By the end of its second year of operation, as a result, the school had nearly forty students. In addition, the first of a small but regular supply of graduate students from good state universities was coming to the school to acquire teaching experience as MacLerren Fellows.

For me, it was all thrilling and tremendously fulfilling. I suddenly had a permanent professional base for myself. As the school's founding director, I taught classes, oversaw the operation of the facility, and found time to push forward with my own painting as well. It was hectic and crazed and exhausting—and I loved every minute of it.

It soon became evident that I was on a roll of good fortune. One winter afternoon during the art school's third year of existence, I received a phone call from Richard Randolph, the chairman of the art department at Southwest Missouri State in Springfield, offering me a position as artist-in-residence at the university for a three-year term. Professor Randolph had served as one of the judges for the Springfield Armory show four years earlier, and he'd been impressed with my work— so much so that he immediately thought of me when the artist-in-residence position opened up. (I later found out that he was under pressure from his superiors to select a woman for the position, which had previously been held exclusively by men.)

The offer was an astonishing opportunity. It came with faculty status and an assistant professor's starting salary, modest but enough to provide for a comfortable standard of living in a place like Springfield. I would be expected to teach a graduate workshop or two, make myself available to students, and devote the rest of my time to my painting. The university's art museum would also sponsor an exhibition of my work during my third year in residence. For an obscure young Ozark artist like me, the appointment was guaranteed to bring visibility and prestige, an *entrée* into the professional art world. Any up-and-coming artist would have killed for it.

But it also meant that I would have to relocate to Springfield, a hundred miles from Plainfield, for the next three years. I would either have to leave my husband and child nine months of the year for three long years or they would have to uproot themselves and go with me. Suddenly,

I found myself confronted with the fundamental dilemma that professionally ambitious young women in the twentieth century so often faced—what do I put first: my career or my family?

When I broke the news to Micah and Jared at supper that evening, I could immediately tell that they were less than thrilled. "You mean we're going to have to move to Springfield?" Jared asked. "Or are you going to go and leave us here?"

Micah cleared his throat and said slowly, "Well, it's obviously a tremendous opportunity for you, but three years is a long time to be away from the farm or live apart. And Springfield's too far away for you to commute back and forth from Plainfield. So what are you proposing to do?" His voice had a sharpness to it that I wasn't used to hearing.

"I don't really know," I said weakly.

"Well, please let us know when you *do* know," Micah replied with what I detected was a trace of sarcasm. I could tell he was upset. As he got up and walked out of the kitchen, I heard him mumble to himself: "I'm not sure this is really fair. I think we've been more than patient and understanding and helpful. . . ."

Later that evening, Jared came to me and asked, "And what about our art school? What's going to happen to *it*?"

"It would go on . . . ," I answered vaguely.

Micah jumped in. "Oh? How . . . ?"

"I'm not sure," I responded. "Besides, I haven't accepted anything yet. But it *is* an amazing opportunity and I *do* feel incredibly flattered to have been asked."

"No question about that," Micah conceded. "But you have to consider the consequences for all of us. And just when we've finally gotten everything in place and our lives are running so smoothly. When do you have to give Randolph your answer?"

"I've got a week or so."

"Well, it's *your* decision," Micah said coolly. "We can't make it for you."

"No, but obviously I'm not about to make such a serious decision without having the two of you on board."

"Let us know what you decide," Micah said with a sigh. "You know Jared and I would never stand in your way . . . ."

Things were tense and cool in the house for the next day or two as I considered Randolph's offer. Micah wasn't his usual warm and cordial self. And Jared was more subdued and standoffish than I'd ever known him to be. I felt as if I was running the risk of seriously alienating my closest loved ones.

It was clear to me that I was facing a pivotal decision— one that would undoubtedly affect the rest of my life. Did I really want to give up all that I had built here in Plainfield in order to advance myself professionally? What if I ended up sacrificing Micah and Jared's love and our family's harmony for personal ambition, for a dream that might never even come to anything?

And was it a dream that I really even wanted?

It would have been one thing if I was Georgia O'Keeffe, living alone and without children, with a staff to see to my needs and a husband as influential as Alfred Stieglitz to constantly promote my work while I made a name for myself. Or if I was Andrew Wyeth, whose wife took care of him and his children, managed his business operations, and marketed his work, so that he was free to devote himself full time to his painting.

But I wasn't an O'Keeffe or a Wyeth. And even if I had been, did I really want the loss of privacy or the other stresses that would come with fame?

The next few days were hell. During the daytime, I kept weighing my options and struggling over what to do. At night, I'd lie awake in bed beside Micah while he slept, listening to him breathe and yearning for our customary closeness.

It was too much for me. One night, I broke down in tears. Micah woke up and turned to me. "I don't want to leave you," I sobbed. "I don't want to leave you and Jared or our farm and everything we have here. I love you! I'm devoted to you! I thank my lucky stars for you! And the center's a dream come true. How can I turn my back on that? How could I ever look Clarissa Billington in the face again?"

The next morning, I called Richard Randolph and turned down his offer. He was disappointed but said he understood. Over the phone I could almost hear him thinking to himself: "This is what happens when you offer the position to a woman with a family."

It was a hard decision, but for me it was the right one. Most ambitious career women would probably have made a different choice. In the fairy tale, the successful modern woman gets to "have it all"—career and family, status and love, fame and fortune. From that perspective, some would say that I had squandered a once-in-a-lifetime opportunity, that I had compromised my career prospects for the sake of my husband and son, that I had rejected modern feminist principles in favor of a traditional male-centered living arrangement.

But I didn't look at things that way. The more I thought about it, the more I began to realize that, in a small-scale way at least, I already had it all. I had a challenging new career as the director of a small local art school. I lived on a beautiful farm equipped with a studio of my own where I could continue my painting for the rest of my life. And I had my own little family—a husband and child whose happiness meant more to me than anything else in life. I was also now firmly settled in the town I had grown up in—a place that I knew intimately and loved dearly—surrounded by scenic rural beauty and by rustic people who were endlessly fascinating and artistically inspiring to me.

I had found my niche in life, and I was supremely comfortable in it.

What more could a woman ask?

Reflections

I CELEBRATED MY SEVENTIETH BIRTHDAY this morning, sitting on my farmhouse porch—peacefully, quietly, and alone—with a cup of coffee and a homemade apple-streusel muffin. It was sunny and unusually warm for a late April morning in the Ozarks, and I felt like being outdoors, delighting in the turn of the weather after a hard, cold winter and a raw early spring.

Looking out over my gardens and barn and the rows of apple trees budding out in the orchard beyond, I found myself thinking about the paths my life had taken and the seventy years that had flown by in such a blur. It seemed like a good time—an appropriate time—for reflection, for thinking about what it all meant.

I thought first about my years as the head of Plainfield's Billington Art Center, and how, over four decades, it had grown from a tiny teaching studio for a handful of local school kids to become a significant presence in the cultural life of our community. After a few years, as the center's painting and drawing classes became more and more popular, I'd recruited a few area craftspeople to offer some basic instruction in pottery-making, wood-carving, basket-making, and weaving. Eventually, we secured a grant from the local chamber of commerce to add an extension onto our building, providing us with more studio space as well as a small multipurpose gallery for exhibitions and public presentations. Soon we were exhibiting the work of local painters and artisans and photographers, and occasionally inviting interesting regional writers, musicians, and dancers to the center for readings and performances. People in town and in neighboring communities began paying attention to our announcements of upcoming events. After twenty years of existence, we changed our name from the Billington Art Center to the Billington Center for the Arts.

As the center expanded its operations, my administrative responsibilities eventually began to wear me down. And so six years ago—could it be that long already?—I semi-retired as the center's director, turning the day-to-day duties of running the place over to Abby Rogers, one of our former MacLerren teaching fellows and a talented artist in her own right. Abby had fallen in love with the center—and with the Plainfield area—during her semester in residence, and she ended up marrying an art teacher from the local high school. She was well-organized and knew lots of people in the art world around the state. As a result, transferring the center's directorship over to her proved to be a seamless transition— although I still stop by every couple of weeks or so to check on things and see if she needs any help organizing an event or curating an exhibit.

As I basked in the morning sun, my thoughts also turned to my career as an artist—although as things turned out, "career" probably isn't the best choice of words. Early on, I experienced a string of successes. Some of my Ozark portrait paintings were included in prestigious public exhibitions, garnering favorable reviews and earning me modest recognition as an innovative young regional artist. Several of the paintings were purchased by private collectors, and a few of them found permanent homes in museum collections and university art galleries in Missouri, Arkansas, and other neighboring states.

But I never broke through to become a famous, nationally known artist. My style of regionalism gradually fell out of vogue within the elite circles of the art world in favor of hyper-realism, neo-expressionism, and other newer genres. I also consciously closed a promising door to potentially Bigger Things when I decided to turn down an appointment as artist-in-residence at the state university in Springfield in order to remain rooted with my family in Plainfield.

I continued to paint, focusing as before on evocative Ozark scenes and subjects. By the time I was in my forties, however, as I concentrated more and more of my energy on running the local art center and looking after my home and family, I could feel my creative spark beginning to dull. My new paintings were technically proficient, but they were increasingly derivative of my earlier works—less original, less edgy. I still produce a new work or two every year, but I find that I'm now painting more for my own personal enjoyment than for public exposure or critical acclaim.

Looking back on it all, I take a considerable amount of satisfaction and pride in what I achieved. From unpromising beginnings, I managed to become an artist, an accomplished painter with at least a modest regional reputation. At the same time, I also got to share my creative passion for art with two generations of local youngsters as an instructor at the Billington Center. And all this while enjoying a full, rich family life with a wonderful husband and stepson. As the kids in the art center would put it: "How cool is that?"

But most of all, as I sat contemplating the past on this beautiful April morning, I thought about the good, unselfish people who had helped me along the way, people who at several key points in my life showed me how to overcome my fears and insecurities and vulnerabilities and develop a sense of self-worth and self-confidence—people who, although scarred by life themselves and with their own problems to worry about, took the time to take a young Ozark girl under their wing and teach her about life, helping her to make her way in the world and make something of herself.

There was Jared Tyler Morrison—Mr. M—who came into my life when I was a scared, confused little girl of nine and quickly introduced me to the therapeutic rewards of making art. An odd, scary-looking man and local recluse who was viewed suspiciously by his neighbors in Plainfield as the town's "boogeyman," he almost single-handedly nurtured me back to health, both physically and psychologically, after my mother's death, and he continued to support my development as an artist for the rest of his life.

There were the Harrises—Ruby Bea and her husband, Doc—an older couple who welcomed me into their lives when I was an early-adolescent basket-case of insecurities and self-doubts—even though they were struggling at the time with Doc's ever-worsening infirmities and a growing lack of respect from his former medical colleagues. Ruby Bea became almost a second mother to me, helping me improve my appearance and self-esteem with her mature womanly advice, while Doc taught me important life lessons about trusting my judgment when we were trapped in a crippling winter blizzard.

There was Madelyn MacLerren, my high school art teacher, who saw hidden talent in me as an artist and went above and beyond the call of duty to help bring it out, despite the fact that she had only recently extricated herself from an abusive marriage. She was instrumental in getting me into the Art Students League in New York City after high school, and she later helped me obtain my first teaching position, back in Missouri, despite the fact that she was dying of breast cancer at the time.

And there was Clarissa Billington, who volunteered her invaluable services to help me get my Plainfield art school up and running. More than anything else, Mrs. Billington provided me with a model for how a small woman—in her case an elderly, crippled widow in a wheelchair—could be tough, assertive, and in control in a man's world.

They're all gone now—all those lovely, generous people. Together, they taught me that the most important thing you can do in life is to give of yourself, to help those in need who can benefit from your friendship and support. It was clear to me, looking back, that the best way to honor them, the best way to thank them for their generosity and aid, is by remembering them and keeping their memory alive.

Gone, too, is Micah, my husband of more than forty years, who died two years ago from acute leukemia at the age of eighty. His death was by far the most devastating loss I have ever experienced, and memories of our life together are interwoven throughout everything I see and think and do. My grief is still too raw for me to try to review our life together in any detail. I'll just say that we had an almost idyllic marriage—one based on deep love, mutual support, encouragement, companionship, and camaraderie, spiced up by an enduring physical attraction and lust for each other, even as we grew older. He was my greatest joy.

In the weeks before Micah died, our son Jared visited several times, flying in from Seattle, where he is a successful architect with a family of his own. He was a tremendous help with the funeral arrangements, and he now calls me weekly to check in and make sure I'm all right. But his life is now in Seattle and mine is in Plainfield, and I'm determined never to become a burden.

A couple of months ago, I received a phone call from Claire Burgess, the head of the Plainfield Children's Services facility, asking if I knew of anyone who could help a 15-year-old girl in their care who was expressing an interest in photography.

The girl—her name was Jessie Culpepper—had been living in the Children's Services group home for two years. The details of her background were a bit murky. There was something about a drug-addicted mother, an abusive stepfather, and a brood of children packed together in a trailer in a rough backwoods area ten miles south of town. Teachers at the Plainfield Middle School had become alarmed by the girl's erratic school attendance, and even more by her appearance and behavior when she did show up for classes: bruised and unkempt, seriously malnourished and painfully shy, dressed in dirty, threadbare clothes. They called the local authorities to investigate, and Jessie was placed in the Children's Services home at age thirteen. She'd been there ever since. According to Claire, she was bright, got good grades, and, in spite of her family upbringing, was "a good girl."

The Billington Center had recently hosted a traveling photography exhibit, "Barns of Taney County," by Robert Cartwright, the chair of the photography department at the University of Missouri in Columbia. The Children's Services staff had taken some of the group home's girls to the exhibit as a special treat. And according to Claire, Jessie had been fascinated by the photos—carefully examining each one in detail at close range and from different angles. As the other girls loaded themselves into the van for the drive home, she had raced back into the center to pick up an exhibit brochure to keep.

After the outing, Claire decided to let her play around with an old Kodak Brownie camera they found in the office storage closet, and she'd taken a roll of pictures with it, mostly of birds and squirrels in the trees outside the group home. Claire believed it might be something worth pursuing and thought of me. Did I have any suggestions?

I told her that I didn't know anything about photography but that I'd be happy to meet Jessie. We agreed on a time the following afternoon at the group home. Before the meeting, I stopped by Plainfield's bookshop and picked up an inexpensive paperback copy of *Fundamentals of Photography*.

When the girl came into Claire's office, I was jarred by what I saw. She was about my height, lean, and sort of sinewy-looking. Her sandy brown hair hung long and stringy, and her bangs hid too much of what appeared to be a rather pretty face. After two years in the group home, she still had a hungry, half-starved look about her, and there was something wary—slightly feral—about her posture and body language. "A wild child," I thought to myself. And yet there was also something strangely familiar about her.

"So, Jessie, do you like school?" I asked her.

"It's OK," she murmured almost inaudibly, her eyes fixed on the floor.

"Mrs. Burgess tells me you're interested in photography."

"I guess," she whispered, still staring downward.

"What interests you most? What do you take pictures of?"

"I dunno."

"Well, here's something that I thought might be of use to you," I said, handing her the book on photography.

Her eyes seemed to light up as she took the book from me. "Thank you," she stammered, and I immediately sensed that I was dealing with a kid who wasn't used to receiving gifts.

Claire told her to show me the snapshots she had taken with the Brownie, and she handed them to me shyly. They were nicely framed, showed an awareness of lighting, and seemed to capture basic aspects of her animal subjects' behavior. "These are very good," I told her. "Keep at it and let me know if the book was helpful."

Over the next few days, I couldn't get the girl out of my mind. On an impulse, I checked out used cameras on the internet, and found an inexpensive refurbished Nikon digital in good condition that I couldn't resist buying for her. When I dropped by Children's Services and gave it to her, she seemed overwhelmed and teared up as she struggled to express her gratitude. "This is a girl who hasn't been treated very well," I said to myself.

"If you like," I told her, "I'll be happy to drive you out into the countryside one afternoon this weekend, so you can take some shots of farm animals and wildlife. The spring bird migration is getting underway, and there should be lots of geese and ducks on the ponds." Jessie said she would like that very much.

The weekend drive quickly turned into a regular weekly event. Jessie seemed to come alive as soon as she was out in nature. Whenever I stopped the car so she could photograph an animal—a sheep or cow, a rabbit or deer, a butterfly, a local songbird or a migrating waterfowl—I noticed that she seemed to have a special knack for getting up close to her subject without scaring it off or spooking it. When I asked her about it one day, she told me she knew a lot about animals. "We didn't have a TV in our trailer," she said, "and I spent a lot of time outdoors in the woods and fields watchin' the critters that live there. And I learnt a lot from Pa when he took me huntin' and trappin' with him."

I also noticed that the photographs she took often had an interestingly direct style to them. Whenever she could, she tried to take face-to-face frontal shots of her subjects looking straight into the camera. This produced a sort of eerie quality in some of her pictures, almost as if she was peering into the animal's soul. In one of her photos, a cow stares directly at the viewer with a look in its eyes that seems to be saying, "What are you going to do to me?" In another, a red-winged blackbird sits on a fence post looking almost accusingly at the viewer as if to say "Stop destroying my habitat." Maybe I was reading way too much into the pictures, but—hey—isn't that what good visual art is supposed to do: let the viewer find his or her own meaning in the image?

Intrigued, I sent a few of Jessie's photos to Bob Cartwright up in Columbia to see what he thought. Bob said her work showed potential and suggested that she might want to look into the ten-week photography workshop that the university sponsors for high school students every summer. "They only admit twenty or twenty-five students per year," he told me. "They have some financial-aid awards available, including a couple of need-based scholarships. It's pretty intensive and competitive, but she might have a chance. Of course, she'd have to submit examples of her best work to the admissions committee. And, oh, by the way, I'm on that committee."

I should probably stop writing now, because Jessie's coming over in a little while to have me help her select the photos for her application portfolio, and I want to be sure I'm ready for her. Later, I'm going to take her clothes shopping.

Acknowledgments

THANKS FIRST to Joseph Carbone, Grace Loo, and Randy Taran, who read early sections of the manuscript, and to James Carbone, Gitane Demone, and Alison Davis for their enthusiastic interest in my work.

Special appreciation to Janis Butler Holm for her wise counsel and unfailing support and encouragement.

Loving tummy rubs for my golden retriever, Maxwell, whose companionship and joie de vivre kept me going through the ups and downs of the writing process.

Eternal gratitude to my husband, Michael Grow, who made this book (and so much else) possible.

And finally, many thanks to Linda Roghaar and the team at White River Press for bringing their high professional standards to the production process.

An earlier version of "Filling In for Mama" appeared as "Geese" in *The Labletter*, 14th edition, 2012.

An earlier version of "Strides in the Snow" appeared as "Coming to Terms" in *Dappled Things: a quarterly of ideas, art, & faith*, 11: 3 (2016).

About the Author

*C*atherine Grow, a former Women's Studies instructor at Ohio University, is a writer living in a small 18th century house that she shares with her husband in rural Connecticut. *The Evolution of Hallie Jo Everheart* was heavily influenced by the decade she spent living as a "back to the lander" in the southern Missouri Ozarks, an experience that has been a deep source of inspiration for much of her fiction.